"Oh my

Kristen was barely aware of anything but the tiny baby on the screen, its knees tucked up to its chest, cozy and secure with not a care in the world, while her heart raced with the enormity of what she was doing.

That little defenseless baby was hers, from its ten tiny, perfectly formed fingers to its miniature toes. Tears stung her eyes and she blinked rapidly.

As her eyes stayed riveted to the screen, the baby's hand moved toward its face as if waving, and Kristen's heart clenched with a surge of instinctual love. In that moment, the fact this pregnancy was real hit her in a tidal wave of emotion, leaving her breathless with joy, fear and anticipation.

She hadn't created this tiny miracle all by herself. And as much as she'd prevaricated over the dilemma of whether to tell Nate or not, seeing the living, breathing evidence of the life they'd created left her with no choice.

Suddenly Kristen knew it was time to give Nate the news. This wasn't only about her, and a good mother always put her child's needs first.

It was the right thing to do.

Dear Reader,

Romance is a huge part of my life. I write it, I read it, I live it. From receiving a surprise bunch of flowers to creating a truly sigh-worthy happily ever after for my characters, I'm a true romantic.

I grew up reading Harlequin Romance® novels, captivated by the dashing heroes, the feisty heroines and the sheer rush of falling in love. I wanted to be a part of it. I wanted to write the type of stories that put a smile on my face every time I closed the book with regret. Luckily, I've achieved my dream of writing the books I love.

Speaking of which, Kristen Lewis and Nathan Boyd are two characters with secret dreams of their own. Can a high-powered executive stay at the top of her career and be a great mom? Can an incredible man who has lost so much already take a chance on love again?

Kris and Nate face a world of challenges, but with romance on their side, they can't lose!

I hope you enjoy reading *Executive Mother-To-Be* as much as I enjoyed creating it.

Long live romance!

Nicola
www.nicolamarsh.com

NICOLA MARSH

Executive Mother-To-Be

TORONTO • NEW YORK • LONDON
AMSTERDAM • PARIS • SYDNEY • HAMBURG
STOCKHOLM • ATHENS • TOKYO • MILAN • MADRID
PRAGUE • WARSAW • BUDAPEST • AUCKLAND

ISBN-13: 978-0-373-17498-0
ISBN-10:   0-373-17498-5

EXECUTIVE MOTHER-TO-BE

First North American Publication 2008.

www.eHarlequin.com

Printed in U.S.A.

From bump to baby and beyond....

Whether she's expecting or they're adopting, a special arrival is on its way!

Follow the tears and triumphs as these couples find their lives blessed with the magic of parenthood....

We have lots of babies on the way in Harlequin Romance:

Expecting a Miracle
by Jackie Braun—April 2008

His Pregnant Housekeeper
by Caroline Anderson—May 2008

Her Baby, His Proposal
by Teresa Carpenter—June 2008

Don't miss Nicola Marsh's next
Harlequin Romance®
The Desert Prince's Proposal
Coming in July!

CHAPTER ONE

KRISTEN LEWIS had a thing for hotels.

She loved the luxury, the hustle and bustle, even those tiny toiletries designed to slather and splurge and make a weary soul feel like a million dollars for that split second in time.

But most of all she loved the anonymity, that people from all walks of life passed by without knowing or caring why a successful thirty-five-year-old woman would be sitting alone at a bar sipping a spritzer.

'Men,' she muttered, stabbing at the lemon wedge in her glass with a swizzle stick, wondering if their ability to blow off other people was a genetic thing.

Even as friends they couldn't be trusted.

She took another stab at the piece of lemon—which was starting to resemble Swiss cheese with the number of jabs she'd taken at it in the last five minutes—as she glanced around the Oasis bar of the Grand Hyatt hotel in Singapore.

She loved this place, with its sleek chrome lines, trendy black furniture with the occasional splash of red, and had spent many hours here with clients and work colleagues during her four-year stint working at a

Singapore TV station. The hotel's grandeur screamed 'special occasion', the reason why she'd chosen to meet Nigel here tonight, envisioning a fun evening with her best work buddy, celebrating the completion of her latest project.

Unfortunately, Nigel had had a better offer from a twenty-two-year-old temp and had given her the brush-off in the foyer.

'Buddy my butt,' she muttered, taking a sip of her fa-vourite white-wine-and-soda combination as her gaze locked with a guy sitting at the other end of the bar.

Not bad flashed across her mind as she took in his dark eyes, dark hair, slight bump in the nose, which added character to his model-handsome face, and sardonic ex-pression highlighted by the slight quirk of his lips.

Dropping her gaze quickly, she returned to studying coasters while mentally listing Nigel's faults, the main one being that he preferred a romantic evening with a bimbo over a night out with a long-term friend. Not that she should be surprised. If Nigel had a choice between wining and dining his latest prospective conquest or sharing a drink with a friend, she'd lose every time.

Letting her gaze sweep the room again in a general fly-by, it unerringly zeroed in on the good-looking guy, and she prepared for a quick look-away. From past ex-perience, guys who looked like that sitting alone at a bar would still be staring at her, trying to make eye contact before moving in for the kill.

Instead, Mr Handsome was staring morosely into his drink, a sombre expression on his striking face, and crazily she sighed in disappointment. She'd never believed in fate or karma or any of that airy-fairy rubbish—yet when she'd locked gazes with the guy a second ago something intangible had zinged between them, almost like kindred spirits meeting and shaking hands before fading away.

Now he wore the same brooding, gloomy expression which matched her mood perfectly, and for an irrational moment she wondered if she should go over there and share sob stories with him.

Shaking her head, she finished off her spritzer—there had to be more wine than soda in it for her to be contemplating such an uncharacteristic action—and scrummaged in her handbag for money.

'Is this yours?'

Looking up from the giant, cavernous hole which sucked up purses, tissues, pens, make-up and everything else she needed on a daily basis, making them vanish with a flick of its clasp, she stared into the darkest eyes she'd ever seen.

A dark chocolate, they stared at her with polite interest, as if expecting something from her.

'Is this your coat?'

His voice washed over her as deep and mysterious and impressive as his eyes, and she blinked, realising he did expect something from her: an answer.

'Oh. Yes, thanks. Was it on the floor?'

She couldn't look away, lost in his hypnotic stare, floundering when she would usually have given Mr Handsome a confident smile, a polite nod and terse reply.

He was probably pulling some slick, practised move on her, and she gave guys like that short shift. Instead, she stood there like a mannequin, stiff and wide-eyed, unable to shake the feeling that this guy was on her wavelength.

Smiling, he nodded. 'Yes, you knocked it off the back of your stool while searching in that suitcase of yours.'

'Suitcase?'

If his eyes had mesmerised her, they had nothing on his smile, which had her surreptitiously leaning against the bar for support.

He pointed to her handbag. 'Looks big enough to store the odd suit and a pair of shoes or two.'

She laughed, and snapped the suitcase shut. 'I'm on the go a lot, so like to have everything at my fingertips. You know, important stuff, like pens and notebooks and all the other paraphernalia I couldn't possibly find anywhere if I left all this at home.'

His smile widened but somehow it didn't reach his eyes, a flicker of sadness darkening their depths to almost black, and she felt another twinge, an uncharacteristic urge to reach out and comfort him. 'Speaking of being on the go, I should catch some sleep. I've got an early plane to catch tomorrow.'

'Here on business?'

'Yes.'

'Ah, too bad for you that it's just a short trip,' she blurted, filled with a desperate urge to keep him talking, to find out more about the mysterious guy who saved ladies' coats from death by trampling, yet wore an invisible cloak of sadness around his broad shoulders.

'Emphasis on "for me"? By your Aussie accent, I assumed you were here on business too.'

'Not exactly. I could be on holiday,' she said, hating the stilted conversation they were having standing up, which was exactly why she didn't usually hang out in places like this.

'You're not on holiday.'

She raised an eyebrow, surprised by his matter-of-fact tone. 'How do you know that?'

'Because holidaymakers have a relaxed look about them, an excited glow, and you don't have it.'

'Gee, thanks. So I've lost my glow too,' she muttered, wondering what she was doing here, making small talk with a guy she didn't know and who'd only stopped because she was a klutz.

'You've got a glow,' he said in a tight, strangled tone which made her look up and register the fleeting interest in his eyes. 'Just not a holiday one.'

Kristen didn't know if it was her bruised ego courtesy of being stood up by Nigel, the spritzer she'd had on an empty stomach or the nebulous connection she felt for this sad stranger, but she found herself doing something completely out of character.

'If you're not too tired and can hold off on the z's a while longer, maybe you'd like to hear about my non-holiday glow?'

He didn't move, surprise mingling with something else in his eyes—regret, hope, desire?—and she wished the ground would open up as heat surged into her cheeks.

'Look, don't worry. I'm sure you have more important things—'

'I'd like that,' he said, hanging her coat over the back of the stool and holding it out for her.

'Great.'

She sat down, baffled by her behaviour and the simple pleasure derived from his acceptance.

'Would you like a drink?'

'A lemon, lime and bitters, please.'

If the splash of wine in the spritzer had been responsible for her erratic behaviour, she'd better stick to the soft stuff otherwise there was no telling what she might do.

After placing their order with the waiter—who had a knowing smile, like he'd seen this scenario a thousand times before—Mr Handsome turned to her.

'I'm Nate.'

Smiling, she held out her hand. 'I'm Kris. Non-holidaymaker. Living in Singapore and loving it.'

Warmth enveloped her hand as he shook it with a solid grip. She liked that. She hated it when guys gave her the limp-fish handshake because of her sex, though she usually showed them, turning their condescension into awe when she wowed them in the business arena.

'Family reasons?'

She shook her head, wondering if he was fishing for info about a significant other, before ditching the idea.

Nate seemed too up-front to play those sort of games. If he were interested he would've asked, and sadly she had a feeling he was sitting here chatting to her out of pity rather than desire for her as a woman. Something in the way he'd looked at her when she'd invited him to share a drink, as if he'd have liked to refuse but didn't want to hurt her feelings.

Oh well, she didn't care. Right now it felt good to talk to someone, especially with a guy who looked like Nate, regardless of his motivations for sitting here with a sad case like her.

'No, I don't have much family. Two sisters back in Sydney, that's it. I've been here working, producing one of Singapore's travel shows.'

'Sounds interesting.'

He thanked the waiter as their drinks were placed in front of them and signed the bill, giving her ample opportunity to study him.

White business shirt unbuttoned at the collar and rolled up at the sleeves revealed strong forearms, and shirt tucked into the waistband of black trousers encased long legs ending in a pair of designer shoes. However, the clothes weren't the interesting part, it was the body beneath: lean, streamlined, a physique hinting at subtle strength.

Very, very nice.

Usually, she wouldn't have given a stranger the time of day, let alone have invited him to share a drink, yet there was something so…so…*haunting* about him, an underlying vulnerability that had her wanting to cuddle him close and pat him comfortingly on the back.

'Can I ask you something?'

Her gaze snapped up from somewhere in the vicinity of his collar, where it parted to reveal a tantalising V of tanned skin, an expanse of skin she found infinitely fascinating for no other reason than what it hinted at, as the rest of his chest filled out the shirt rather well.

'Sure.'

'You were muttering into your drink earlier. Is everything okay?'

Once again, heat seeped into her cheeks. Could this get any more embarrassing, the gallant guy having a pity drink with the desperately ditched girl?

'You know what they say about talking to yourself being the first sign of madness? Well, I'm mad all right. Mad enough to want to throttle my buddy Nigel for bailing on me.'

'Ouch.'

Nate winced and she squared her shoulders, ready to rebuff his pity. Instead, she saw a glimmer of amusement lighting his eyes. 'Did he stand you up?'

'Sure did, the louse. Said he had a better offer from this girl he's been chasing for a while, so he ditches a friend for a bit of fluff. Nice.'

'Very poor form,' Nate said, his eyes twinkling beneath a mock frown. 'Friends should always come first.'

He was making light of her situation and, rather than being insulted, laughter bubbled within her at the big deal she'd made out of something pretty insignificant. 'Why did you think he stood me up?'

Nate's amusement spread to his mouth, tilting it upwards at the corners. 'Well, one look at that bag and the maniacal gleam in your eyes, any man would've made a run for it.'

She laughed, surprised the annoyance of being stood up by Nigel had receded, replaced by an unexpected need to share confidences with this guy.

'Ah, but you didn't. You're sitting here, aren't you?'

'Good point.'

He tipped his glass in her direction before taking a long sip of beer, his gaze never leaving hers.

She couldn't figure him out.

He wasn't flirting with her or making suggestive comments, or even hinting at anything untoward, but when he stared at her like that—steady, unwavering, loaded—the air between them sizzled with an invisible current, and had her reaching for her own drink which she gulped down in record time.

'You know it's his loss, right?'

Breaking the hypnotising eye contact, she said, 'Yeah, I know. The guy's got his priorities all wrong.'

'So he wasn't the love of your life?'

Kristen snorted, picturing scruffy, laid-back Nigel as anything other than a work buddy she could offload to at the end of a rough day.

'No way. Nigel and I are purely platonic.'

'Then he's definitely not worth worrying about now. You can give your friend an earful when you next see him.'

'Too right.'

Suddenly, she realised how trivial her complaint against Nigel was, and wanted to know more about the sadness she'd glimpsed in Nate when she'd first seen him. 'What about you—any life stories to tell?'

If she'd doused him with her icy drink she would've got the same response: shock combined with pain, sorrow quickly masked by an enforced blank mask.

'Not really. I'm married to my job; don't have time for anything else.'

'I know the feeling,' she said, trying to cover her monstrous gaff in prying into things which didn't concern her. 'Just call me Mrs TV Producer. So, what do you do?'

He hadn't lost his shuttered expression, and he waited before speaking, as if weighing up every word. 'I'm involved in the entertainment area too, though on the business side of things.'

'So you're one of the corporate bigwigs who control the purse strings, right?'

At last, a glimmer of a smile. 'You could say that. I'm the CEO of my own company and, apart from handling sporting rights for everything from rugby to the Olympics, we branch into other areas too.'

'Well, if I ever need a job I'll know who to come to,' she said, hating how her mind immediately latched onto his use of the word 'handling', and conjuring up startling images of him doing exactly that…with her!

'You do that.'

He drained his beer and she braced herself for the inevitable parting, totally confused by her reluctance to let him go.

She didn't know this guy.

She didn't want this to end.

She didn't have the foggiest idea what to do.

'I'm hungry after that beer. Do you want to join me for dinner?'

Trying to hide her relief—and elation—she said, 'That would be great. The buffet here is the best in Singapore.'

'So I've heard. Come on, let's try it.'

Sliding off her stool, Kristen ignored her voice of reason which yelled *What do you think you're doing, having dinner with a guy you barely know? Are you nuts?*

'I don't usually do this type of thing,' he said, handing her the infamous coat. 'Having dinner with women I just met.'

'That makes two of us.'

Happily ignoring her voice of reason, she sent him a shy smile and headed for the restaurant.

Nate forked a delicious combination of spicy black-pepper crab and fried rice into his mouth, trying to concentrate on the amazing food on his plate rather than the intriguing woman sitting across the table from him.

What am I doing here?

He'd asked himself the same question repeatedly over the last half hour and still hadn't come up with an answer. One that made sense, that was.

He didn't chat up women, he didn't accept drink invitations in hotel bars, and he sure as hell didn't have dinner with them unless it involved business, yet here he was sharing the best meal he'd had in ages with a beautiful woman he'd known for less than an hour. And enjoying it!

'Good?'

He nodded, his gaze fixed on her mouth and the way her lips wrapped around a crab claw, his groin tightening at the sheer eroticism of the movement.

This couldn't be happening.

He usually didn't have the time or the inclination. So what was he doing, fantasising about this virtual stranger's lush mouth and what it would feel like on him?

'I'm a seafood addict,' Kris said, dabbing at her glistening mouth with a serviette while he wrenched his mind out of the gutter. 'This place is famous for it.'

'Along with the roast duck, tandoori chicken, satays and the million other dishes on offer, you mean?'

She smiled, the power of that one simple action staggering in its ability to capture his interest and keep him riveted. 'Wait till you try the desserts.'

He didn't have a sweet tooth in his body, but suddenly he couldn't wait to try a chocolate mousse or lychee sorbet. In fact, he'd go along with anything this fascinating woman suggested at the moment, which showed exactly how jet-lagged he must be.

He needed to stop these two-day jaunts to Asia if this

was the result: a confused, half-drugged state which had him focussing on all the wrong cues, like the way her stunning blue eyes sparkled, how the highlights in her short, layered blonde hair shone and the way her smile lit up the room.

As for her body—tall, lithe and graceful in the slim pinstripe skirt and pale-blue shirt—he'd been struggling not to stare since he'd first seen her hunched over that gigantic bag of hers in the bar with her jacket in a pool at her feet.

She'd appeared deliciously rumpled and flustered when he'd picked up her coat, and nothing like the ice-cool blonde who'd locked gazes with him a minute before with her big, sad eyes and grim expression.

He'd watched her for a while, toying with her drink, stabbing at the lemon wedge, her mouth muttering words he couldn't hear. He would've laughed if her expression hadn't been so fragile, and, though he'd had his own problems to deal with, he'd been unable to walk past her without reaching out and giving her some indication that she wasn't alone in the world, some indication that he understood.

Boy, did he understand.

People said grief eased with time, that time healed all wounds.

People didn't know jack.

'You know, dessert is optional. You don't have to try it if you don't want.'

Hating the realisation that his mask had slipped for a moment, and she must have glimpsed some of what he was feeling, he said, 'Sorry, just thinking.'

'About something not very pleasant, by the looks of it?'

The question hung between them, softly probing but intrusive nonetheless.

'Guess being away from home has me in a mood.'

'Being homesick is the pits,' she said, replacing her serviette on the table and sitting back. 'I missed Sydney like crazy when I first came here, but you want to know the secret to getting past it?'

'Sure.'

Leaning forward, she tapped the side of her nose as if about to depart a secret lost in time. 'Orang-utans.'

Maybe the jet lag was worse than he'd thought. He could've sworn she'd just said something about home-sickness being cured by great apes.

She nodded, a smile playing about her mouth. 'You heard me. Orang-utans. The biggest, goofiest guys on the planet. You can't help but love them. I was feeling pretty lousy my first week here, so I took a trip to the Singapore Zoo and spent an hour with the hairy goofballs, having breakfast with them, laughing at their antics. Suddenly, no more homesickness. Instant cure, just like that.'

She snapped her fingers and he blinked, wondering what it was about this cool yet kooky woman that had him so captivated.

'I'll keep that in mind,' he said, shaking his head in disbelief, torn between wanting to bolt from the table before she enthralled him any further and hauling her into his arms to see if she was real.

She flitted between serious and funny, sad and happy, changing emotions like the frenetic activity of the stock market on opening.

He hardly knew a thing about her, yet he wanted to know it all.

He didn't know her surname yet he knew she loved seafood, had a brain behind her beauty, and had a thing for big, orange apes.

They had little in common, yet he suddenly knew he didn't want this evening to end.

He wanted to know more, he wanted her with a staggering fierceness that clawed at him, begging to be let out and soothed by her touch, in her arms, all night.

'Uh-oh, you're having more of those unpleasant thoughts.'

She picked up the wine bottle and topped up his glass, as if a fine Shiraz would fix what ailed him. If it were that easy, he would've bought out every vineyard in Australia by now.

Direct to the point of bluntness in business, he took a deep breath, opting for the same approach now and hoping it didn't earn him a thundering slap.

'Actually, my thoughts aren't so unpleasant.'

'Oh?'

Her eyebrow kicked up, highlighting the curious glint in her blue eyes.

'I know this is going to sound crazy, and you have every right to walk away from this table when I've finished, but I was just thinking how we have a connection and I don't want this evening to end.'

Surprise flashed across her face, closely followed by—indignation?

Fear?

Hope?

He had no idea. It had been a long time since he'd spent this much time with a woman, let alone tried to fathom her emotions.

'Are you asking me to spend the night with you?'

Put like that, he tried not to cringe. It looked like he wasn't the only one who favoured the direct approach.

'I don't know what I'm asking,' he muttered, eyeing the door and wondering if it was too late to make a run for it. 'I don't do this very often. Hell, I haven't been out with a woman for years. But I know one thing—I'm attracted to you. You make me feel good. And I don't want to lose this feeling, no matter how temporary.'

Suddenly, it was as simple as that. No more, no less.

This stunning woman with her expressive eyes and lush mouth had him feeling good for the first time in a long time, and he wanted more.

'I think you do know what you're asking,' she said, her gaze locked on his, her smile uncertain as she toyed with the end of the tablecloth, twisting the damask over and over. 'I think we both do, and my answer is yes.'

'Yes?'

He exhaled, unaware he'd been holding his breath, filled with elation and anticipation and myriad emotions he couldn't describe as she stared at him with excitement glittering in her expressive eyes.

'Yes.'

From that moment everything faded into oblivion as he stood up, held out his hand, experienced an electrifying jolt as she placed hers in it, and led her from the restaurant to the lifts leading up to his room.

They didn't speak.

They didn't need to.

Words seemed superfluous as they entered his room, closed the door and fell into each other's arms like two drowning people hanging onto the last lifebuoy: desperate, frantic, caught up in a storm bigger than the both of them.

As her lips clung to his and he deepened the kiss, his arms sliding around her waist to mould her to him, a thrill shot through him.

He'd never done anything so rash, so reckless, so damn impulsive, and it felt good.

It felt great.

Thanks to the beautiful woman in his arms, he suddenly realised it was time to start living again.

CHAPTER TWO

KRISTEN never did anything on impulse.

She'd never understood the rash decisions people made on the spur of the moment and then lamented later. She was a thinker who weighed up options carefully for everything, from buying a pair of killer black stilettos to hiring the best grip boy.

Yet here she was lying next to the sexiest guy she'd ever met after having amazing sex. Twice!

Logical? No.

Well thought out? Uh-uh.

Satisfying, cataclysmic and exciting? Oh yeah!

Wriggling under the cotton sheet covering them, she stretched, tensing every muscle from her toes to her fingers, before relaxing, savouring the warm, sated sensation creeping through her tired body.

To say she'd never felt like this before would be the understatement of the year.

Risking a quick glance at him, she smiled, lost in delicious memories of how he'd kissed her, held her and made love to her with every inch of his body, and corny as it might sound, she knew it had been more than a physical connection.

Quite simply, they'd clicked.

For whatever reason—whether it had been his underlying vulnerability, his innate sadness or the fact he was a refined, well-mannered, genuinely nice guy—she'd thrown caution to the wind and made love with a virtual stranger.

She should be mortified, or cringing with embarrassment at the very least. Instead, she rolled onto her side and watched him sleep, filled with a calmness she'd never known.

With his lips relaxed into a half smile, and his long, dark eyelashes fanning his cheeks, he looked a lot younger than when he'd been awake and carrying around the inherent sadness like a backpack weighing him down.

What would make a successful, wealthy guy who looked like he could model underwear on billboards around the world so sad?

Guys his age with money to burn were usually chasing women, striving for the next big thing, and whooping it up in general—not necessarily in that order. She should know; she mixed in those circles and held those players at arm's length constantly.

Yet here was a guy who probably moved in that social sphere wearing his sadness like a badge of honour. He appeared to be a loner, not that she really knew anything beyond the basics about him. Heck, she didn't even know his surname!

However, there was something about him… She hadn't conjured up their connection out of thin air. It was there, it was real, and for the last few hours everything else had faded into the background while she'd linked up with a kindred spirit.

Weird, whacky, but true. No one would believe her, but then who would she tell?

'You're awake.'

Blinking away her memories she focussed on Nate, smiling at his heavy-lidded, half-asleep expression.

'Can't sleep. Guess I'm not used to sharing my bed.'

Ain't that the truth!

Not that it bothered her. She valued her independence, and hated having to fight over the duvet with a guy hogging half the bed.

'Whose bed?'

He smiled, his tone, soft and husky, washing over her like a warm spring shower and making her want to throw her arms wide and dance from the sheer beauty of it.

'Good point. Make that *your* bed,' she said, wondering how this could feel so right.

She'd expected a tense, awkward conversation on waking, perhaps the odd excuse or two. Instead they lay there, grinning at each other like a couple of goofy teenagers, barely inches apart, buck naked.

'You're okay with all this, right?'

His smile waned as the light in his eyes faded.

Uh-oh, here goes the whole 'this was a mistake, see you around' chat.

She nodded, making sure her smile didn't slip. 'Of course. I wouldn't be here if I didn't want to be. We're two consenting adults, we made a decision to spend the night together. No big deal.'

Then why the empty ring to her words? Or the hollow feeling in her heart, when she had no right to feel anything other than physical attraction for this guy?

'You're right,' he said, dropping his gaze to her hand bunching the sheet, and she relaxed with effort.

He might have just agreed with her mature, rational assessment of a rather awkward situation, but the guilty expression ripping across his face said otherwise.

She could've reached out to him, prompted him to tell her what was wrong, but she didn't have the right. In fact, apart from sharing one fabulous night of scintillating sex and an unexpected connection, she didn't even know him, at least not enough for him to share confidences with her.

Still wanting to ease the sadness now mingling with the guilt on his expressive face, she said, 'Look, I don't usually do this sort of thing, and by your reaction I'm guessing it's the same for you.'

He raised his gaze slowly upwards, remorse darkening his eyes to almost black. 'I never do this sort of thing. Why, does it show?'

Great, now he thought she'd insulted his prowess!

Reaching out to him, she covered his hand with hers, hoping the simple physical contact would convey half of what she was feeling.

'Last night was fabulous. I just meant that dealing with all this aftermath stuff is kind of icky.'

'Icky, huh?'

His lips twitched, and she silently congratulated herself for bringing a smile back to his face.

Returning his smile, she said, 'I guess what I'm trying to say is you've got nothing to feel bad about. We both wanted to be with each other last night, let's leave it at that.'

His smile flickered as something akin to shame

flashed in his eyes, and she knew she'd somehow said the wrong thing again.

'You're an incredible woman, Kris. Thank you for last night.'

He reached out and cupped her cheek, his thumb brushing her bottom lip in the slowest, most tender, barely-there movement before letting go, leaving her wanting more, craving his touch when she hardly knew it.

This wasn't good.

She was neither drunk nor stupid, so lying here lost in useless wishes of 'what may be' was pointless.

Nate had a plane to catch and a life to get back to, she had a new job in Australia to look forward to.

Time to start looking to the future, and chalk up this incredible encounter to a fate she didn't believe in.

'Thank you,' she said, brushing a hasty kiss across his lips before slipping out of bed, clutching the bottom sheet around her. 'You have a plane to catch in a few hours, so I'll leave you to it.'

'Kris?'

She paused, wishing she could skip the farewell and fast-forward to when she'd be back on solid ground, away from the seductive powers of a virtual stranger in an exotic place, caught up in the type of magical romance she knew didn't exist in the real world.

'Yes?'

Nate stared at her, his dark, intense gaze trying to send her a message she couldn't fathom. Once again his sad mask had slipped into place, and for a split second she wondered if their impending goodbye had anything to do with it.

Yeah, like he'd be heartbroken over a woman he barely knew.

'I wish things were different.'

For one heart-stopping moment, she felt the same zing, the same spark she'd felt back in the bar when they'd first met, the same tenuous connection that this was right, was meant to be, and she almost ran back to the bed and flung herself into his arms.

But that wasn't the sensible thing to do, and right now logic was about all she had left.

'I do too,' she finally said, opting for honesty, yet knowing it wouldn't make a difference as she slipped into the bathroom to get dressed and head back to her well-organised life and out of his.

CHAPTER THREE

KRIS strode up to the shiny chrome desk of Channel RX, feeling every bit the new kid on the block and hating it. No matter how confident she was, or how carefully she chose her clothes, she always felt the same terrifying insecurity she'd felt every time she'd started a new school or been introduced to a new foster family. And that had been way too many times for her liking.

Pasting her sparkly toothpaste-smile on, she leaned on the desk and fixed the young receptionist with a confident stare. 'Hi, I'm Kristen Lewis, the new executive producer.'

The receptionist, a young version of Julia Roberts, held up her hand as she fielded what looked like five calls at once as the switchboard lit up, and Kristen relaxed, feeling at home straight away.

At least this wasn't any different. She could walk into any television studio around the world and find the same harried receptionist, the same flood of incoming calls from irate or scandalised viewers, and a buzz out on the studio floor you just couldn't beat.

She loved working in television: the drama, the rush, the constant push to be better and strive higher than the competition. She was good at what she did, which was why she'd been lucky enough to land this plum job at Melbourne's premier station.

She couldn't wait to take up the challenge, something new to take her mind off Singapore, and that fateful night she couldn't forget no matter how hard she tried.

'Right, sorry about that. I'm Hallie, general dogsbody around this place. Would you like to head on through, or shall I call the boss and let him know you're here?'

'I'll find my own way, thanks. Give me a chance to look around.'

Hallie sent her a relieved smile as she cast a frantic look at the switchboard which had lit up like a Christmas tree again. 'No worries. If you need anything, holler.'

Kristen waved and headed for the imposing black swing doors.

This was it.

The start of a new job, life in a new city without the complications of memories of a guy with unforgettable dark-chocolate eyes.

'Kristen?'

She stopped and swivelled to face Hallie. 'Yes?'

'The boss man just buzzed through to ask if you'd arrived. He wants to see you in his office asap. Through the doors, down the corridor on your left, last office on the right.'

'Thanks.'

Kristen pushed through the doors and into the swankiest studio she'd ever seen. Polished floorboards lined the endless corridors stretching left and right, with countless doors off each one, while straight ahead lay a huge auditorium-like space enclosed in glass with a small army swarming around a mock-kitchen set.

No one stopped to stare at the new girl, not even to give the odd curious glance. She knew what it was like. Once the cameras were set to roll it was heads down, bottoms up, as everyone performed their roles to perfection. The cameras didn't lie, and the slightest mistake could cost a whole take or, worse, be aired live to an unforgiving audience.

A tingle raised the hackles on her skin, and she shivered. Damn, she loved her job.

Feeling more confident with every passing second, she headed off down the left corridor as instructed, resisting the urge to peek into every office. Many doors were wide open, the hum of voices and the smell of brewed coffee heavy in the air, and she hoped her new boss would offer her a cup. She'd kill for a caffeine hit right now, what with the move to Melbourne on top of her recent sleepless nights—courtesy of Mr Handsome, who she really hoped would turn into Mr Forgettable any time now.

She knew nothing about her new boss. After having been headhunted by a producer here at RX, she'd barely had time to study the channel's prospectus as she'd rushed around like a maniac, wrapping up her work and life in Singapore, let alone learn who the head honcho was.

Thankfully, she rarely dealt with the CEOs of outfits like this: slick, go-get-'em types who were focussed on the bottom line and little else. She'd much rather concentrate on the enjoyable task of creating great TV than counting the behind-the-scenes wheeling and dealing.

Reaching the final door on the right, she pulled up short.

'Nathan Boyd, CEO'.

She blinked, hating the irrational surge of heat the name Nathan sent through her.

Damn it, she should be over this, over him.

It had been one night, nearly three months ago, for goodness' sake! One incredible, amazing night when she'd connected with a guy whose surname she didn't even know.

Yeah, really connected.

Shaking her head, she wiped her damp palms against her skirt, tugged at her jacket hem and, swinging her bag over her shoulder, she rapped sharply at the door.

However, as the door opened and she willed her legs to stay upright, Kristen knew forgetting Nate and that one eventful night would be impossible.

Totally impossible considering Nathan Boyd, CEO—Nathan Boyd, her new boss—was her Nate.

The guy who had rocked her world.

Nate's smile faded as Kristen tried her best not to reel back in shock.

'Kris?'

Not the smoothest of opening lines, but then considering she couldn't think let alone form words at that moment he was faring a damn sight better than her.

Looking way too calm, he stepped aside and gestured her in. 'Please come in.'

She ignored his invitation, her legs rooted to the spot. Wasn't he the least bit rattled to find her on his doorstep? How could he look so cool, so unflappable?

Suddenly, white-hot anger shot through her as she studied his composed face, knowing exactly why she'd been headhunted for this job, and by whom.

'I don't believe this!' she finally blurted, years of pro-fessionalism deserting her as she stared at him in growing horror, heat surging to her cheeks.

'Come inside and we'll discuss it,' he said, his voice as deep and steady as she remembered as he opened the door wider and waited for her to step inside.

Marching through the door like a woman sentenced to the gallows, she collapsed into the nearest chair on the visitor's side of his desk, and took several calming breaths before she exploded.

'Did you know about this?'

Taking a seat behind his desk, he sat back, shoulders relaxed and arms resting comfortably on his fancy leather director's chair, while she could barely keep a lid on her growing temper.

'About you working here? No.'

'Really? I'm guessing there aren't a lot of executive producers named Kristen. Were you behind me being headhunted?'

'Why would you think that?'

Rolling her eyes, she said, 'Come on, you're a smart man. Do I need to spell it out? Singapore—the night we were together?'

His lips thinned into a compressed line as he ran a hand through his hair, the first sign he was anything other than on top of the situation.

'Look, I had no idea who the new exec producer was till I opened that door and saw you standing there. I've been in charge of this operation less than twenty-four hours, and have spent most of that time out on the studio floor. I haven't studied employee lists, haven't had the time. Instead, I've asked Hallie to send along everyone from the top down at half-hourly intervals so I can get acquainted face to face rather than studying boring CV's.'

'Uh-huh,' she said, her anger somewhat deflating at the sincerity in his voice as the reality of the situation finally hit her.

She'd just barged into her new boss's office with the finesse of a wounded rhino, flinging wild accusations and acting like the injured party, when in fact this was her dream job and she could've just botched it with her erratic behaviour.

'I'm surprised you didn't do your homework. You know, study up on who you'd be working for.'

Nate fixed her with a stare she found disconcertingly familiar, a gleam of challenge in the dark depths of his eyes, and she bristled, hating his implications that she wasn't professional.

'I did. Though I guess the contract I signed or the prospectus I read didn't mention your name.'

She snapped her fingers, not willing to give him an inch, her latent anger taking little to reignite. 'Then again, I wouldn't have made the connection, not knowing your surname and all.'

He stiffened, the faintest red staining his tanned cheeks. 'You're overreacting. You don't see me throwing around allegations, like maybe you knew I was CEO here and wanted to give me a shake-up by walking in here today as my newest employee?'

'Overreacting?'

She leaped from her chair before she could think twice, planting her hands on his desk and leaning forward.

'Aren't you the least bit thrown by this nightmare situation? Don't you feel awkward? And do you honestly think I'd go to the trouble of faking a shocked reaction just to get a rise out of you?'

Shaking her head, she plopped back down in her chair, suddenly embarrassed by her outburst. 'Look, I'm sorry if I did overreact, but honestly finding out you're my boss has thrown me.'

Though, in all honesty, not half as thrown as how attracted she was to him even in a crazy situation like this.

While she wanted to rant and rave at the injustice of having to work with a guy she'd rather forget, she couldn't help but admire his charcoal-grey designer suit and the way it fitted the great body she'd already had the pleasure of exploring in intimate detail.

As for his eyes… They had a mesmerising quality, their darkness a fathomless pool of mystery which begged to be explored, and her pulse raced at the memories of how far she'd taken that exploration…

Sitting back, he clasped his hands behind his head, every bit the consummate professional, while she struggled to refocus her wandering attention and come to terms with her new employer.

'A coincidence over which I had no control. Now, what do you want to do?'

She wanted to walk out of his office and never look back.

She wanted to stop noticing the way his business shirt stretched across his chest as he leaned back, the same hard, muscular chest she'd had one-on-one contact with.

But most of all she wanted to forget how he'd made her feel on that one incredible night.

Taking a steadying breath, she said, 'I want to be the

best damn executive producer RX has ever had. But this is still uncomfortable.'

She waved her hands between the two of them, wishing he wouldn't look at her like that, the intensity of his dark gaze resurrecting memories she'd rather forget, her mind still reeling from the fact they'd be working together.

'It doesn't have to be. We're professionals. I'm sure what's happened in the past doesn't have to affect our work.'

'Professionals. Right.'

Suddenly her shoulders relaxed, and she sat back in the chair, knowing she'd faced a lot hairier situations and come out on top. Besides, how hard could working with Nate be?

'You're right. We both didn't mind the anonymity that night, and it's in the past. Done. Forgotten. So, Nathan Boyd, what's your vision for Channel RX and how do you see me fitting into it?'

Straight to the point and no bull. She liked that in the people she worked with, and hoped he did too, especially considering her rather emotional outbursts since she'd first set foot in this office.

Thankfully, he accepted her switch back to professionalism and, gathering a stack of papers in front of him, he shuffled a stapled bundle into a glossy navy folder and handed it to her.

'My vision's in there, laid out in black and white. I want Channel RX to ultimately be number one in Australia. I want ratings in prime-time slots to soar, I want innovation, I want a fresh slant on old faithfuls such as the news and current affairs. In a nutshell? I want it all.'

'You're aiming big,' she said, a tiny thrill of excitement shooting through her at the thought of working with a boss who had a clear vision. 'I like that.'

Nodding, he clasped his hands and leaned forward. 'As I haven't had a chance to find out from other sources yet, tell me what you bring to RX.'

'That's easy. I'm the best.'

She shrugged, knowing now wasn't a time for modesty. She needed to impress Nate, to wow him, to show him that what they'd shared really was in the past, and she could give one hundred percent to the job despite her earlier uncharacteristic tantrum.

His lips twitched, resurrecting instant memories of how they'd felt, how he kissed, and she quickly subdued that train of thought.

'You're very confident.'

'You have to be in this business,' she said, fixing him with a direct stare designed to convince him of her sincerity. 'I love my job. I'm prepared to put in the long hours, to do whatever it takes to make the shows I work on successful. I demand respect, and I treat co-workers the same way I'd like to be treated. I won't settle for second best. I deserve more than that.'

His lips curved upwards into a genuine smile as he stood and held out his hand. 'I think you'll be a great asset to this station. We're going to make a good team.'

'Thanks.'

She shook his hand quickly, dropping it before she had time to register the quick surge of heat from his palm to hers. 'I'll go find my office and get acquainted with the rest of the gang.'

'Great. I'll see you later.'

She headed for the door, wondering if this surreal experience was a dream and if she'd wake up as soon as she stepped out into the corridor.

'Kris?'

'Yes?'

Her hand stilled on the doorknob as her heart thudded at the way he said her name, at the memories of how many times he'd murmured her name that night in Singapore.

'It's good seeing you again.'

Managing a half-strangled smile, she bolted out the door.

Kristen willed her legs to move at a sedate pace from Nate's office, when in fact she wanted to bolt down the long corridor and keep running till she reached the massive front doors and beyond.

Seeing the guy she'd spent countless sleepless nights trying to forget open that office door had been like a slap in the face, a swift, sharp wake-up call that she hadn't forgotten him at all. Or, more precisely, hadn't forgotten how he'd made her feel: feminine, desired and special.

How could he elicit those feelings when she barely knew him?

How could she face him on a daily basis knowing he had that sort of power over her?

Rounding a corner, she pulled up short as Hallie held up her hands to prevent a collision. 'Hey! You okay?'

Schooling her face into a practised confident mask, she nodded. 'Sure.'

By Hallie's raised eyebrow, she didn't believe her. 'Didn't the meeting with the boss go well?'

'It was fine.'

Yeah, right.

'You look like you could use a coffee. I'm heading to the cafeteria. Want to join me?'

Kristen would've preferred to find her office and get settled in while getting her emotions under control, but the lure of caffeine proved too strong. She needed something to jolt her out of the trance-like shock at finding Mr Handsome was none other than Nathan Boyd, her new *boss!*

'Love to,' she said, falling into step with Hallie, who stood a head shorter than her but moved with the speed of light despite her three-inch stilettos.

'What did you think of the boss?'

Kristen chose her words carefully. 'Nathan seems like a man with a vision. The channel should go far.'

'Nathan, huh?'

Hallie sent her a wink, and Kristen battled a rising blush and failed, speaking quickly to cover her gaff. 'He's very informal for a CEO. Actually, I didn't expect to meet him on the first day. The CEOs of stations I've worked at before didn't get too hands-on, but I get the impression he likes to be quite involved, especially on the creative side.'

'The boss only started yesterday, and if you want my opinion he can get hands-on with me any time.'

'That's not very professional,' Kris blurted, wishing she'd bitten her tongue as Hallie stared at her in wide-eyed confusion.

Thankfully, a group of cameramen greeting Hallie like a long-lost friend defused the moment. Besides, she wasn't jealous. She had to care to be jealous, and she didn't, she couldn't.

'Okay, here we are. Welcome to the Ritz,' Hallie said,

waving off the boys and holding open the cafeteria door for her. 'Come on, the coffee isn't bad, if you don't mind the odd dreg or two.'

Smiling at the receptionist's sense of humour, Kristen followed her into a cavernous room filled with stainless-steel tables and chairs, chafing dishes piled high with hot food lining one wall, and a huge selection of crisps, chocolate bars and sodas nearby.

From what she'd seen so far, Channel RX did things on a grand scale, and if the quality of their current shows that she'd managed to watch so far was any indication she'd made a good decision.

'What'll it be? They do a mean latte and, seeing as it's your first day, my shout.'

'Latte's fine. And thanks,' Kristen said, feeling like a chick being pushed around by a mother hen.

'Right, here you go. Let's sit over there, and you can tell me the Kristen Lewis story,' Hallie said, handing her a steaming latte in record time and making for a table in the farthest corner.

'Not much to tell,' Kristen said, unable to resist Hallie's open friendliness, but wary all the same. 'Besides, if I tell you all my deep, dark secrets on the first day, you'll think I'm a gossip.'

Hallie rolled her eyes. 'As if. I've only been here a couple of months, you're new, and so I'm bestowing you the great honour of being my work buddy.'

Kristen didn't know what to say, and before she could come up with something Hallie held up her hand. 'Uh-uh. Don't thank me. I know it's a highly coveted position to be on the good side of the receptionist. I know you're probably shell-shocked but, trust me, I'll be nice.'

Staring into Hallie's guileless blue eyes, registering her wide, friendly smile, Kristen knew that at least she had one ally at RX.

Taking a sip of her surprisingly good latte, she said, 'Are you always this upfront?'

Hallie nodded, her auburn curls bouncing around her face. 'Yep. Only way to be. I know you're an exec and will probably blow me off after this, but hey, no harm in trying, right?'

Kristen fought a rising blush and lost. 'Actually, I've always been a bit of a loner on the job. Too tied up in my work, I guess. But, hey, I appreciate the coffee. If you buzz me any time you're having one, and I'm free, I promise not to blow you off. Deal?'

'Deal.'

Hallie settled back into her chair as if snuggling into a comfy sofa, when in fact Kristen knew the hard, cold steel chairs were there to discourage occupants from getting too cosy and encourage them to get back to work pronto. 'So, what's your background?'

'I've worked in Singapore the last four years, London for a while, brief stint in LA, and before that Sydney, which I guess I call home. Worked my way up to executive producer through those jobs, loved every minute of it.'

'Wow, sounds glamorous.' Hallie's eyes lit up, and Kristen wondered when she'd last had that wide-eyed interest in anything. 'But you've basically given me a run-down of your CV. What about your personal life? Any goss there?'

Determinedly ignoring a fleeting image of a naked Nate which flashed across her mind, she forced a laugh and made a grimace. 'Not so much, I'm afraid. I'm a confirmed workaholic. Single and loving it.'

Hallie sent her a dubious look, but continued her grilling anyway.

'Why Melbourne? Why RX?'

'The station has a stellar reputation in the industry. I wanted to come back to Australia, and the opportunity knocked on my door so I took it. Now, if you could spare me a minute in this interrogation, I'd like to have this latte before it goes cold.'

She'd meant it as a joke, but it looked like her buddy skills were on a par with her maintaining-a-relationship skills, as Hallie's face fell.

Darn it; she knew there was a reason she didn't do the friendship thing. Being direct was the only way she knew, and treading around bruised feelings was foreign to her.

She guessed she'd better learn fast if she didn't want to alienate the one person who'd been genuinely nice to her in the last week.

'Sorry, didn't mean to sound so harsh. I'm a bit strung out with the move to Melbourne and starting the new job.'

'No worries,' Hallie said, her resident cheery smile slipping back into place. 'I have to get back to work anyway. I'll save the rest of the interrogation for later.'

'Later?'

She'd envisaged a long day getting acquainted with the running sheets, her co-workers and the station in general. She'd have no time for further coffee breaks, especially ones fraught with probing questions from a girl just trying to be friendly.

Hallie snapped her fingers. 'I forgot, you probably don't know about Manic Mondays.'

'Actually, I think I do,' Kristen deadpanned, knowing the frantic rush of a new working week all too well.

She usually grabbed a bite to eat at her desk for dinner, working all hours to get the week's scheduling on track. It had been the same at every station around the world, and it was comforting to know things weren't so different around here.

'Bet you don't.'

Hallie's sly grin piqued her curiosity, and she grabbed her latte, falling into step beside the petite receptionist.

'Okay, enlighten me.'

'Every Monday everyone stops work at eight and convenes to our local bar for a bit of team bonding and boosting of morale. It's great.'

Taking time out of her busy schedule to have a drink at a bar with co-workers on a Monday night? As if.

'I'm sure it is, but I'll be tied up tonight.' And for every Monday night while she worked here.

She didn't do the casual socialising thing well, preferring to maintain a distance with work colleagues. Sharing a coffee with Hallie was a first, and if the girl knew she'd probably label her a freak.

Not that she cared. She'd been labelled a heck of a lot worse growing up, and she'd survived.

'I'm betting you're not.'

Hallie held open the door and Kristen walked through, sending her one of her characteristic 'don't mess with me' looks. 'Why's that?'

Hallie leaned forward as if about to impart a trade secret. 'Because Manic Mondays are company policy. Everyone goes, from the janitors to the CEO. It really does keep everyone happy. The first drink is on the house, and if people want to stay around they do, but mostly everyone has a drink or a coffee, a bit of a chat, then heads home. It isn't a super-late night, and the powers that be find it works as well as a bonus scheme for morale.'

'Right,' Kristen said, feeling like she was in quicksand and floundering.

Since when did the powers that be sanction weekly social get-togethers for employees, let alone make it mandatory? And *everyone* had to attend?

She'd have a chat to the CEO about this. Just as soon as she plucked up the courage to face him without wanting to fall into his arms.

CHAPTER FOUR

NATHAN sipped at his espresso, content to lean against the bar away from the RX crowd and watch. You could learn a lot about people by the way they interacted with others, and seeing his employees mingle and chat spoke volumes.

Like Hallie, the young receptionist, whose bubbly personality won over everyone within two feet. And Alan, his second in command, who alienated everyone with his pompous ramblings, yet nobody moved away for fear of offending a bigwig.

Then there was Kristen, a fish out of water if ever he saw one. The erect posture, the fixed smile, the glazed look in her striking blue eyes, and the fact she kept casting furtive glances at the door told him she didn't want to be here.

He'd picked her as a fellow loner in Singapore, but he'd expected a confident career woman like her to be more outgoing, more extroverted, yet right now she looked like she'd rather have teeth pulled than stand around and mix with her new workmates.

Draining his coffee, he set it on the bar and made his way towards the door. He'd done his duty, putting in an appearance when all he'd wanted to do was head home and read the pile of reports tucked into his briefcase.

However, getting to the door put him straight in the path of the one woman he'd rather avoid and had done a good job of doing so far.

'Kristen.'

'Nathan.'

Their polite nods and flat tones grated on his nerves, especially when she'd previously called him Nate. In Singapore he'd shocked himself when he'd told her his name was Nate, when it had been an abbreviation reserved for Julia and close family, yet once it had slipped out he hadn't minded. He'd liked how it had sounded on her tongue, how natural it had seemed, lending a familiar quality to what should've been a once-in-a-lifetime chance meeting.

Instead, here they were again, trying their utmost to act like they hadn't spent an incredible evening chatting and joking before indulging in the surprising passion which had consumed them both.

'Heading home?'

'Loads of work to do. You know how it is.'

'I sure do,' she said, a spark of understanding in her blue eyes creating an instant bond between them. 'I guess we're both finding our feet in a new job, huh?'

He nodded, torn between escaping while he still could and staying a while longer in the hope of getting their relationship—their working relationship—back on an even keel. 'It's tough at the start, but I actually love walking into a new place and starting fresh. It's a challenge.'

Kris smiled, the first time he'd seen a genuine expression since their inauspicious beginning earlier that day. 'And, let me guess, like any male you thrive on a challenge?'

'Nothing wrong with that.'

He returned her smile and their gazes locked. He should've looked away first, but he couldn't, riveted by the tiny flecks in her deep blue eyes, remembering how they'd glowed and sparked when she'd been warm and eager in his arms.

Thankfully, she finally broke the deadlock with a little laugh. 'No, there's nothing wrong with enjoying a challenge. I'm all for it myself.'

'The go-get-'em businesswoman, huh?'

'That's me.' She raised her glass in his direction. 'Don't say I didn't warn you.'

'I stand duly warned,' he said, looking forward to seeing what this dynamic woman could bring to his life. To his *working* life.

She sipped at her drink, a teasing glint in her eyes as she lowered it. 'Good. Because I intend to put in the long hours, do the hard yards, whatever it takes to take RX to the top, just as my pushy boss wants in his vision statement.'

He chuckled. 'So you read the documents already? I'm impressed.'

'You ain't seen nothing yet.'

Suddenly, her smile faded, and he wondered at the turnaround, wishing he could recapture some of the easygoing camaraderie of the last few minutes.

'It's great to have an employee with a vision too. But won't long hours interfere with your family?'

Being involved with anything other than business

came at a cost, and he should know. He was still paying a steep price.

If her smile had faded moments before, the shutters well and truly came down now as her expression blanked. 'I can't remember if I told you in Singapore, but I only have two sisters. Carissa's based in Stockton, just north of Sydney, and Tahnee's in Sydney. They're both overseas travelling with their families at the moment, so don't worry, I won't have any distractions.'

'Sorry for being nosy,' he said, the coldness in her voice sending a chill through him. So much for camaraderie. 'Just trying to foster good employee relations.'

'Don't worry about it,' she said, waving off his apology, but her flat tone told him he'd botched whatever inroads he'd made in getting her to unwind tonight.

'On that note, I'm definitely heading off.' Before he put his foot in it again, and this time set her off like the wild woman who'd stormed into his office this morning.

'Actually, I think I'll head off myself. If it's good for the boss, it's good enough for me,' she said, her fragile smile creating a pocket of warmth deep within, and he fell into step beside her, heading for the door.

She waved to Hallie, who cast them a curious glance, and he held the door open for her, savouring the light rose scent he remembered all too well. It had lingered on his sheets after she'd left his hotel room, just as imprinted on his brain as the memory of what they'd shared.

'Would you like me to walk you to your car? Inner-city Melbourne can be a bit dodgy at night,' he said, surprised by a strong surge of protectiveness.

He hadn't felt that way towards a woman since Julia, what seemed an absolute aeon ago now.

'My car's right here, so I'll be fine, but thanks.'

'Right. I'll see you tomorrow, then.'

She nodded and crossed the road, an elegant, tall figure in a fitted houndstooth suit, sheer black stockings and towering heels. Dressed for business, she looked incredible, but as hard as he tried he couldn't forget how much more incredible her body was underneath the clothes.

Blinking away that unforgettable image, he waited till she got into her snazzy two-door car, started the engine and pulled away from the kerb, returning her brief wave as she drove by.

He watched till he could make out nothing more than her tail-lights glowing red in the distance, like two glittering eyes pinning him with an accusatory glare.

'Kris, can you come in here now?'

Throwing down her pen on the stack of scripts in front of her, Kris glared at the intercom phone on her desk, hating the thing more than her mobile phone, considering both had become an instant connection to Nate and his demanding ways.

Sighing, she hit the answer button. 'Be right there,' she said, pushing away from her desk and grabbing her personal organizer, a writing pad and the latest updates on new shows, knowing that no matter how prepared she was her new boss would find something to faze her with.

Heading down the long corridor to his office, she smiled at several co-workers, amazed that she'd only been here four days when it felt like a lifetime.

Familiarity bred that feeling. It also bred contempt,

which she was fast heading towards if Nate didn't lighten up a bit.

'Come in,' he barked, a second after she knocked on his door and, fixing a sickly-sweet smile on her face, she strode into his office.

'You wanted to see me, boss?'

His head snapped up like she'd called him something far worse—which wouldn't be entirely out of the question, considering how grumpy he'd been the last few days—and he frowned.

'Take a seat. I need to discuss something with you.'

'No problems.'

She slid onto the chair opposite him, stacking her pile of paper on her lap, and doing her best to appear perky and upbeat, hoping it would highlight how grouchy he was being.

Sitting back in his chair, he crossed his arms, and she struggled not to notice the way his biceps bulged beneath his pale-blue business shirt. In a way, having him act like a pain in the ass was better than having him joking around with her, like on Monday night when it had felt way too comfortable standing in a crowded bar with the man she couldn't forget no matter how hard she tried.

'I want to run an idea past you.'

'Shoot,' she said, clicking her pen and automatically sliding her writing pad to the top of the pile on her lap.

'You remember we discussed a new travel show on Tuesday?'

'Uh-huh.'

How could she forget? They'd been holed up in his office talking over a few ideas for new shows and she'd pushed her own barrow, determined to impress on her second day on the job, well aware of her expertise in the travel-show area. However, what she hadn't been prepared for was the host of memories which had continually scattered across her mind at the most inopportune moments, talk of travel resurrecting Singapore moments, Grand Hyatt moments, long, hot, exquisite moments with Nate...

'I've given it a lot of thought, and I want us to run with it. See what you can come up with and we'll meet to discuss it on Monday.'

'Fine,' she said, unable to keep a huge self-satisfied smile off her face, only to find him glaring at her like she'd just thrown a glass of cold water over him. 'What time?'

Reaching for his personal organiser, he keyed in a few numbers and frowned.

'The earliest I can do is four-thirty. I'm in Brisbane till then.'

'Sounds good,' she said, making a show of checking her own gadget, but knowing she'd shift a meeting with Elvis himself to show her uptight boss what she could do. 'Anything else?'

Okay, so maybe she was laying it on a little thick with her sweeter-than-honey smile and saccharine voice, but the more intimidating he got the more she wanted to push him.

After all, she did enjoy a challenge. And she had warned him!

He stared at her, his dark eyes revealing nothing, but she could've sworn she saw the corners of his mouth twitch. But that meant he wanted to laugh, and there was no way her serious boss would actually crack a smile during work hours.

Shaking his head, he said, 'No, that's it. See you Monday.'

'Have a good trip.'

Striding to the door, she put an extra swivel into her hips, grateful she'd worn her tightest black skirt today.

If Nate wanted to treat his new exec producer with cold indifference, she'd give him a bit of a shakeup and show him that he hadn't always been so impervious to her.

Swivelling at the door, she caught him staring at her butt a split second before his gaze snapped up to meet hers, and his residual frown slipped into place.

'Was there something else?'

Fighting a triumphant grin and losing, she said, 'Never mind. We'll discuss it further on Monday,' and sauntered out the door.

'This is it?'

Kris gritted her teeth to keep from snapping at Nate as he flicked through the documentation she'd prepared, his expression carefully schooled into a blank mask that gave nothing away.

'That's what I've come up with so far. I wanted to outline the gist of the show, run through a few preliminaries with you before getting too involved. What with budgets being the be-all and end-all, I'd like to see what you think before taking it further.'

He nodded and rubbed his chin absentmindedly, flicking the last page shut and finally looking up at her.

'It looks good. I particularly like the reality-show slant you've put on it. It's something new, innovative and exactly the direction I want RX to be heading. Great job, Kris.'

She smiled, instantly forgetting how less than five minutes earlier she'd wanted to pick up the fancy letter-opener on his desk and stab him with it, considering he'd been an hour and a half late, had waltzed in here with his usual sore head and proceeded to read her proposal in silence without giving her a clue as to what he thought.

'I'm pretty excited about it, as you can probably tell,' she said, pointing at the giant stack of paper she'd prepared to wow him with.

Tapping his pen on the stack, he said, 'I'm amazed you did all this since Thursday.'

'Once I got going I couldn't stop.'

Wasn't that the truth, considering she'd spent her entire weekend preparing this presentation rather than enjoying the Melbourne sunshine.

'When you said long hours, you meant it.'

He made it sound like a fault, and she bristled.

'Of course. I'm a professional. I thought you'd gathered that by now.'

A spark of awareness flared in his eyes as he registered her dig.

'Your work speaks for itself,' he said, staring at her for longer than was comfortable before slamming the stack of paper in front of him and making her jump. 'And, speaking of which, I want to nail some of the prelims of this tonight. Are you happy to work back?'

'Sure,' she said, not happy in the least.

Most of the employees had already left for Manic Monday at the local, and while Nate hadn't given her the slightest indication he saw her as anything other than an employee—bar the butt-ogling incident, but she'd basically incited that, and he was only male!—the thought of being cocooned in his cosy office for the next few hours suddenly seemed too intimate when she'd rather keep her distance.

'Good. I'll order in dinner. Chinese okay?'

She nodded mechanically, instantly transported back to that night in Singapore when they'd feasted on fried rice and other Asian delicacies, before feasting on each other.

'Any preferences?'

'I'm not fussy.'

Taking a peek at him from beneath her lashes as he ordered, she wondered if he ever thought about that magical night. Though he was civil to her, he'd gone cold since her first day, almost as if he'd deliberately erected a barrier she couldn't breach.

'Right, that's done. Let's get to it.'

They worked steadily for the next half hour, with Kris making frantic annotations on her paperwork as the ideas flowed between them fast and furious.

She'd worked with some of the best around the world, but bouncing ideas with Nate took creativity to a whole new level, and Hallie's knock on the door almost came as a welcome reprieve as her mind spun.

'Hey, guys, your dinner's arrived.'

Hallie dumped it on the table, took one look at the stack of work in front of them and grimaced. 'I take it you won't be making it to Manic Monday?'

'Afraid not,' Nate said, leaning back in his chair, clasping his hands and stretching, the simple action creating a strange flurry in Kris's gut and bringing a broad smile to Hallie's face.

'Well, then, I'm off.' Hallie turned her back on Nate

and sent Kris a huge wink as she headed for the door. 'Don't work too hard, guys. And don't spend all night with your noses to the grindstone.'

'I'm not that dedicated,' Kris mumbled, the spicy aromas from the takeaway boxes making her nose twitch and her tummy rumble as Hallie closed the door, leaving her all too aware of exactly how good it was to actually spend all night with Nate.

'I think you are,' Nate said, gesturing towards her presentation. 'And your boss is suitably impressed, but why don't we take a break and dig in?'

'Sounds good to me.'

She placed her pen and pad on the table and worked the kinks out of her neck, surprised to find Nate hadn't moved a muscle when she finally looked up.

Instead, a slow-burning heat turned his eyes to molten chocolate as he smiled, the first time she'd seen him send her anything other than a frown for the last week.

'What?'

If his cold treatment left her flustered, it was nothing on how she felt basking under the warmth spilling from his eyes now.

'We're both very driven,' he finally said, reaching for the takeaway cartons and handing her chopsticks, as if the loaded moment had never happened.

'Uh-huh,' she mumbled, shovelling Singapore noodles into her mouth with gusto.

She'd skipped lunch trying to put the final touches to her presentation, and was now starving. By the hungry gleam in Nate's eye and the way he kept staring at her, it looked like she wasn't the only one. Though somehow it seemed she'd morphed from a professional employee, to be kept at arm's length at all times, to an exceedingly tempting morsel.

Okay, maybe that last part was in her own head, but it had a nice ring to it.

'Good?'

He'd barely touched his Kung-Po chicken, while her chopsticks were perilously close to scraping the bottom of her noodle box.

'Fabulous.'

'Almost as good as in Singapore?'

Her heart skipped a beat. Surely Mr Professional hadn't just referred to the one night they'd vowed to ignore?

She could just take the easy way out and opt for a nice, safe answer, the type of answer he'd expect.

But where would the fun be in that?

'Nothing could be as good as that night,' she said, staring him straight in the eye.

He didn't blink.

He didn't look away.

Instead they sat there for what seemed like an eternity, the air crackling between them, bound by the same tension which had made them lose their heads that one magical, balmy night a couple of months ago.

'You're right,' he murmured, taking a stab at a piece of chicken with his chopsticks, unsurprisingly coming up empty considering his eyes hadn't left hers.

In that moment Kris knew that, no matter how cool Nate pretended to be, he hadn't forgotten what they'd shared. Not any of it.

'Well, we better eat up and get back to it,' she said, the false brightness in her voice almost making her cringe.

But she had to do something to get them back on

track, away from the touchy subject of that incredible night and how much she'd like to re-create the same magic again the longer he stared at her with fire in those hypnotic eyes.

'Right.'

In an instant, the heat evaporated, only to be replaced by Nate's cool indifference, and Kris stifled a sigh.

After all, she'd got what she wanted.

Hadn't she?

'Kristen, where are we at with the casting for *Travelogue?*'

Kristen fixed Nate with a glare, convinced he was doing the whole 'let's pick on the new girl' thing on purpose. What with his condescending tone, she could quite easily have throttled him.

'We're on schedule. The final screen tests are done, and we're expecting visa clearance for the last cast member as we speak.'

A tiny frown appeared between his brows and, seeing it combined with his compressed lips, she knew what came next couldn't be good.

'That's all well and good, but what's the actual time frame? Are we talking days or hours here? I need direct answers, not vague platitudes.'

Stiffening, Kristen twirled a pen between her fingers, refraining from stabbing it into her notebook, or better yet stabbing it into the man who had made her working life miserable for the two weeks since she'd started.

She didn't get it.

He'd been fine on her first day, had been the epitome of a chivalrous gentleman, waiting till she'd reached her car after Manic Monday before leaving. Most guys took her confident persona as a sign she could take care of herself—and she could—but it had been nice to feel protected for that brief moment.

However, since that night he'd closed off, and, if she didn't count the slight aberration during their working dinner when he'd thawed for all of two seconds, their conversations had been cold and clipped, his demeanour bordering on antagonistic and she'd had a gutful. Once this meeting was over, she'd confront him.

'The embassy doesn't work to your stopwatch and they can't give me precise times. As soon as the visas come through, I assure you, you'll be the first to know.'

She shouldn't have spoken to him like that, not with Alan watching their sparring with avid interest, but there was only so much she could take and Nate had crossed the line about a week ago with his surly attitude and frigid tone.

'Fine. Let's adjourn till we have more.'

If looks could kill she would've curled up her toes on the spot, but she didn't flinch from his glowering stare.

He could say things were fine, but she knew differently, and she had every intention of finding out what was going on. What had happened to his holier than thou 'we're professionals' speech he'd given on the first day?

Gone as quickly as the special spark she'd imagined they'd once shared.

'Keep me posted,' Alan said, gathering up his paperwork and heading for the door in record time.

Maybe her poker face needed some work, for he cast her several concerned glances on his way out, obviously not wanting to get caught in the crossfire when she let Nate have it.

'Thanks, Alan, shall do,' she said, forcing a smile which quickly faded once the door closed and she turned to face the boss.

'We're finished here,' he said, sliding documents into clear plastic sleeves and shoving the lot into a box he hefted onto his hip.

'On the contrary, we're just getting started.'

She planted her hands on the conference table and leaned forward, fixing him with a glare that had wilted lesser men than him.

'I want to know what's going on.'

'We had a business meeting as far as I can tell,' he said, replacing the box on the table, his exasperation audible.

'Don't patronise me,' she said, hating the tension between them, hating the fact she cared even more. 'You've been giving me a hard time ever since I started. I've done everything you've asked of me and more, yet you can't be civil. What's with that?'

He froze, his expression icy. 'I treat you like any other employee. If you expect special treatment, forget it.'

'Special treatment? Why would you think I'd expect that?'

She knew, though, and the thought sent raw anger spearing through her. Would he ever let her forget the mistake she'd made in Singapore?

'Look, this is getting us nowhere. I'm sorry if you think I've been too pushy or tyrannical or whatever, but it's how I do business. If you don't like it, maybe we need to come to another arrangement.'

'Are you threatening to fire me?'

She gripped the table, her blood pressure soaring and spots dancing before her eyes.

'You're…' The words died on her lips as she swayed, the spots joined by squiggles and stars and quickly followed by darkness as she collapsed onto the table.

Nathan's blood chilled as he watched Kris slump forward in a heap, her head making a god-awful sound as it thumped on the table. He rushed forward in time to catch her before she slid to the floor, struck by two things simultaneously: how scared he was that she'd injured herself, and how petrified he was at how good she felt cradled in his arms.

'Wh-what happened?'

Her eyelids fluttered open, and he breathed a sigh of relief, unaware he'd been holding his breath.

'You passed out,' he said, brushing the strands of hair off her forehead, wishing the lump of fear lodged in his throat would disappear. The longer she stared at him with uncertainty in her wide blue eyes, the larger the lump grew, till he could hardly speak.

'I've never fainted in my life,' she said, her brow creased as if puzzling over what had happened.

'Maybe you've been pushing yourself too hard.'

God knew *he* had, pushing her away every way he knew how.

'I'm used to working at a hectic pace,' she said, shaking her head and wincing as she reached up to feel the growing bump near her hairline. 'Ouch, that must've been some knock.'

'It was. Shook the building, I'd say.'

'Who asked you?'

Her rueful smile faded as her fingers connected with

the bump, and his heart clenched with the fragile glint in her eyes.

'Here, let me check it out.'

He'd expected her to protest, but she surprised him by lowering her hand and closing her eyes as his fingertips skimmed the bump on her forehead and beyond, using gentle pressure to explore her scalp for further damage, relieved he didn't find any.

His relief was short-lived, though, as he registered how damn wonderful it felt to be running his fingers through her hair, just like he'd done that night he'd been trying so damn hard to forget.

Pulling his hand back as if scalded, he gently raised her to a sitting position, needing to get her out of his arms before he did something crazy, like kiss her bump better and follow up with a kiss on her lips to make him feel better.

'You should get to a doctor, get yourself checked out,' he said, propping her against a chair while he reached for a glass of water off the table and handed it to her.

'I hate going to doctors,' she said, taking a sip gingerly before closing her eyes tight again, a pained expression on her face.

'What's wrong?'

'I think I'm going to be sick.'

'Hell,' he muttered, casting a frantic glance around the room for something to act as a sick bag, and coming up empty.

'Just give me a second, it might pass,' she said, taking slow, deep breaths and looking paler by the minute.

Hating the helpless feeling rendering him almost useless, he grabbed one of the clear plastic sleeves containing the month's projection figures and tipped them out in a hurry. It would do as a sick bag at a pinch.

Suddenly, her eyes snapped open, and she fixed him with an accusatory glare.

'Don't think this means we've finished our conversation. As soon as I'm feeling better, you're going to face the music, mister.'

He smiled, relieved to see some of the familiar fire in her eyes, amused that she'd think of chewing him out at a time like this.

'Duly warned,' he said, taking hold of her arm. 'Think you can stand? I'll help you up, then grab a phone so you can call your doc.'

'I don't think—'

'Don't think, just dial. You need a check-up, as I won't stand for having one of my prized employees collapsing on me for no reason.'

Rather than arguing as he expected, she accepted his assistance and he got her onto a chair without further drama, though he should've known she wouldn't stay silent for long.

'If this is how you treat prized employees, I'd hate to see how you treat the ones you don't value.'

Grabbing his cell phone out of the pocket of his jacket draped over the back of his chair, he said, 'Hey, didn't I stop you from falling on the floor in an undignified heap?'

She waved away his response, the colour returning to her cheeks. 'Not that—the way you've been carrying on the last two weeks.'

'We'll talk about that later,' he said, handing her the phone. 'Now, call directory enquiries if you don't know your doc's number off by heart. I'm not letting you out of my sight till you're in a taxi and on the way to see him or her.'

'I don't have a doctor in Melbourne,' she said, thrusting out her bottom lip in a delightful pout which matched her sulky tone.

'Then you can see mine. Doc Rubin is one of the best,' he said, dialling the number and fixing her with a glare that brooked no argument.

'I'm feeling fine now. It was probably the result of long hours and snatched meals.'

'Something tells me you've always worked like that, yet you said you haven't fainted before.'

He waited while the doctor's receptionist put him on hold, hoping he wasn't overreacting.

Maybe she was right and this was a one-off. However, seeing her so helpless lying there with her eyes closed, and cradling her limp body had resurrected stark memories of holding Julia in a similar way. He'd been too late to save her, and he'd be damned if he dismissed Kris's fainting spell out of hand when it could indicate something more serious than overwork.

'You're being awfully bossy,' she muttered, her arms crossed over her chest in an action he'd come to associate with her stubborn side several times during meetings over the last week or so.

'Funny, that, considering I'm your boss.'

He held up his hand as the receptionist came on the phone again, and he took the first available appointment which happened to be in half an hour, courtesy of a cancellation.

Thanking the receptionist, he snapped the phone shut. 'Right. We're all set. Let's go.'

'You're not coming with me!'

Her horrified glance told him exactly what she thought of the idea of his accompanying her, and he stopped short, suddenly struck by how inappropriate it might look for the boss to be seen mollycoddling an employee.

She's more than that and you know it.

Ignoring his inner voice, he said, 'Actually, I was thinking Hallie could ride with you.'

He held up his hand as she opened her mouth to protest. 'Don't even think about arguing. You can't be alone in case you collapse again, so Hallie is riding with you, okay?'

'Okay,' she said, her meek tone telling him exactly how scared she was, but trying to hide it. 'But this doctor better be good.'

Hiding a triumphant grin, he said, 'You'll be in good hands with Doc Rubin. And make sure you head home straight from the surgery. I don't want to see you back here, got it?'

'Is that *ever*?'

He ignored her jibe at their earlier conversation, aware he'd have to do some fast talking once she was better. Anything rather than tell her the truth.

'I'll call you later to see how you went,' he said, offering her a hand to help her up from the chair, which she ignored now she had some strength back.

He should've known her dependence wouldn't last long. She'd never accept a helping hand from him unless desperate.

'Do you need a hand to the front door?'

'I'm fine.' She stopped short of rolling her eyes, and he grinned, holding his hands up in surrender.

'Don't think this lets you off the hook. I'll be back to bust your butt faster than you can say "that's a wrap".'

'I'll look forward to it,' he said, thinking that for a woman who acted so tough she had a delightful sense of humour, and he much preferred being on the receiving end of a funny barb than the killer glare she did all too well.

Then again, he'd done such a good job of alienating her, maybe busting his butt wasn't a joke!

Keeping her at arm's length was proving to be more difficult than he'd anticipated.

Perhaps he had to try a whole lot harder.

CHAPTER FIVE

'YOU'RE pregnant.'

Kristen stared in horror at Dr Rubin, who was a dead ringer for Santa Claus. Ironic, considering she'd never believed in fairy tales or the jolly fat guy himself, especially as he'd never brought her what she wanted. No surprise that his lookalike delivered shocking news she didn't believe.

'There has to be some kind of mistake,' she said, folding her arms and fixing him with a withering stare.

The doctor shook his head, a kindly smile on his rotund face. 'No mistake, Miss Lewis. Can you tell me the date of your last period so I can calculate your due date?'

Right then, the first flicker of doubt set in.

Last period…

When had that been?

She'd attributed her missed periods to changing time zones, the move to Melbourne and the stress of a new job. It wouldn't have been the first time she'd missed a period or two at a tough time in her life.

Never in her wildest dreams—or nightmares—had she considered she could be pregnant.

Racking her brain, she said, 'Over twelve weeks ago? I'd have to check for the exact date.'

'We can go into that later, but right now let me give you a rough estimate.'

While the doctor twirled a cardboard circle peppered with numbers, she sank into the chair and furiously tried to marshal her thoughts.

She couldn't be pregnant.

She didn't know the first thing about being a mother, let alone caring for a child.

How on earth had this happened?

Suddenly, an icy shiver spread cold, clammy fingers through her body. She hadn't slept with anyone apart from Nate, which meant…

'Your due date is December the first.'

'Oh no,' she sighed, squeezing her eyes shut and shaking her head from side to side in a futile attempt to vanquish the logical explanation as to who the father of the baby was. 'No, no, no…'

'I hate to state the obvious, but this pregnancy is un-expected?'

Her shocked gaze met the doctor's understanding one, and she hated the anger bubbling within her at the futility of her situation.

A baby had never been in her grand plan. She had a career, a successful life, she didn't need the complication of a child and all the responsibility he or she entailed.

Darn it, they'd used protection. How could this have happened?

Rubbing a hand across her eyes, she tried to erase the all-too-vivid image which flashed across her mind in response to that particular question.

'We can discuss options if you don't want this baby,' Dr Rubin said, his voice devoid of emotion or judgement.

She didn't want to discuss options.

She wanted to run screaming from his office, head home, dive under her duvet and hide away from the truth: pregnant, to her boss!

Taking a deep breath, she slid a protective hand over her flat belly. She needed time to think, time to absorb the shock, time to figure out what she wanted to do, though in reality she knew it would take a lifetime to get used to the idea of herself as a mother—and Nate as her child's father.

Lifting her chin, she met the doctor's concerned stare. 'That won't be necessary.'

'Good. In that case, let's discuss obstetricians. You'll need to have your first review and ultrasound asap, as you're probably nearing the end of your first trimester.'

'Fine,' she said, knowing it wasn't.

Making the decision to be a mother was one thing, facing up to specialists and ultrasounds and goodness knew what was another.

Apart from knowing next to nothing about kids, she didn't have the faintest idea about what pregnancy entailed—apart from the obvious, like nausea and swollen ankles and a belly the size of a basketball. She had no friends to ask, and the thought of going through this alone hit, and hit hard.

Though there was Nate…

Nate, the father of her baby, who could barely bring himself to look at her these days, let alone acknowledge that the one night he'd made clear meant nothing to him had resulted in a baby.

How could she tell him something like this?

How would he react?

God, what a mess.

'Right. Here's a list of obstetricians, and the multi-vitamins I recommend you commence immediately. Any other questions?'

Kristen stared at the doctor. Was he crazy? She had a heap of them, starting with *how bad will the labour be?* and ending with *how will I care for a baby?*

However, she swallowed her questions and shook her head. If she spent one more minute in this doctor's office, with his twinkly eyes and benevolent smile, she'd start blubbering and never stop.

'No, I'm right for now. Thanks for your help.'

She stood quickly, grasping the information he'd thrust at her to her chest like a shield, and made for the door.

'Miss Lewis?'

She paused and turned back. 'Yes?'

'Congratulations. Bringing a baby into this world is a truly wonderful experience.'

Easy for him to say. He was a man.

She managed a grim smile, which must've come out more like a grimace, and tore out of the room, stuffing the information into her handbag, desperately craving fresh air and a reality check.

'Hey, wait up!' Hallie called out, and she forced her feet to stop.

She needed time to compute what the doctor had just told her, and if her overzealous friend got wind of her predicament the news would travel around RX with the speed of a film on fast-forward.

'What's wrong? Are you all right?'

Kristen nodded, knowing nothing would ever be right again. 'Some viral bug.'

Hallie's eyes narrowed as if she didn't believe a word of it. 'Why were you tearing out of here like a bat out of hell?'

'Fresh air.'

Kristen fanned her face, pretending a slight stagger, and Hallie made a 'be right back' sign at the medical receptionist and hauled Kris outside before she collapsed.

Taking in deep breaths, and feeling like the worst kind of fraud for deceiving the closest person she had to calling a friend, Kristen braced herself against a stubbly brick wall.

'Must be some virus to make you faint,' Hallie said, her head cocked to one side like a curious sparrow.

'Mmm,' Kristen mumbled noncommittally, wondering when she legally had to inform RX about her condition.

Her condition.

She'd hated hearing pregnancy labelled that way in the past, like it was an illness and not a natural part of life. The women she'd worked with had been having babies, not suffering from some debilitating sickness, yet colleagues had blamed the slightest thing—from a missed meeting to a late memo—on their 'condition'.

She hadn't fought it back then, not deeming it relevant, but boy did she have a different outlook now. The first person to label her with a 'condition' would get slugged. Though that could just be the irrational hormones kicking in and making her want to slug anybody, including the infuriating guy who'd got her into this predicament in the first place.

'Ready to go back inside? I'm sure that beady-eyed woman thought we were running out of there without paying. Typical receptionist!'

Hallie rolled her eyes, and Kristen laughed for the first time in hours.

Hopefully, she could be that self-deprecating when the time came for her to face the inevitable sly comments about her pregnancy.

Suddenly grateful for Hallie's presence, she reached out and squeezed her hand. 'Thanks for being here. You've done nothing but make me feel welcome since I started at RX, and I really appreciate it.'

Hallie blushed. 'No worries. For an uptight exec, you're okay.'

'Enough with the compliments.' Kristen matched her smile, and turned back towards the medical centre before swinging to face Hallie. 'Can you do me a favour?'

'Sure.'

'Let Nathan know I'm fine? I think he kind of freaked out when I fainted in that meeting, and said he'd ring me later, but I just want to head home and go to bed.'

'No worries, I'll tell him,' Hallie said, bristling like a protective feline before continuing. 'He's a great boss, though, isn't he? Not many bigwigs would take an interest in their employees like he does.'

Kristen stilled. Was Hallie fishing for info? Had she sensed a past connection between Nate and herself?

'I've worked with worse,' she said, keeping her voice devoid of emotion, hoping to nip Hallie's possible fishing expedition in the bud. 'Now, let me pay this bill, organise taxis for us and head home. I'm beat.'

'Okay.'

Hallie didn't push the issue, and Kristen attributed her comments to the run-of-the-mill frank statements the receptionist was famous for.

Hallie thought the boss was great?

Well, Kristen would soon find out if that was true once Nate heard that his newest executive was pregnant.

More importantly, that he was the father.

'Though I'll share the taxi to your place, then head home from there.'

Kristen opened her mouth to argue, but Hallie held up a hand. 'It's not open for debate. Besides, this may be the only chance I ever get to boss you around.'

Hallie winked, and in a small way Kristen was happy to have the company home. Chatting to Hallie might keep her mind off her predicament—for all of two seconds.

She paid the bill and called a cab, her head spinning the entire time, and thankfully Hallie kept up a steady stream of conversation until they reached her place.

However, as soon as she laid eyes on her terrace house, a thousand doubts plagued her: could she bring up a child in a place like this? Was it too small? What about the steep stairs—and the split-level lounge? And her totally impractical furniture?

'Kris, are you okay?'

Hallie covered her hand with hers, and with that small, caring gesture Kristen snapped and burst into tears.

Not dainty tears, but huge drops which trickled down her cheeks at the speed of light and plopped onto her cream linen skirt, accompanied by sobbing and hiccups and the works.

'I'll take it from here,' Hallie said, thrusting the fare

at a bemused taxi driver and assisting her out of the taxi like an invalid.

'I'm sorry,' Kristen murmured, trying to stem the tears, only to find they flowed faster as she unlocked her front door and stumbled into the hallway.

'Hey, don't apologise. Viruses can make us do strange things.' By the dubious look on Hallie's face, she didn't believe the virus story for a second. 'Now, sit down and I'll get you something to drink. What would you like?'

'Water, please. Kitchen's through there.'

'I'll find my way around,' Hallie said, casting her a concerned look before hurrying away, giving Kristen valuable time to regain control.

She never cried. Ever.

She'd had plenty of opportunity in the past thanks to her upbringing, but tears had been seen as a sign of weakness by bullies, and she'd soon learned to never give them an inkling of her emotions.

Now, it looked like the floodgates had opened and wouldn't stop in a hurry.

'Here you go.'

Hallie thrust a tall glass of water into her hand and plopped onto the couch next to her, waiting till Kristen had drained most of it and her tears had subsided before speaking.

'You know I'm your friend, right?'

Kristen nodded, surprised to find she did consider Hallie a friend. They'd bonded over a few coffees at work, and she'd almost blurted the sorry tale about Nate's cold treatment several times but had stopped at the last minute, aware that loose lips sunk executive producers' ships.

However, if ever she needed a friend, it was now.

'In that case, why don't you really tell me what's going on?'

Kristen opened her mouth to fob Hallie off, to repeat the virus story, to give her any number of false platitudes.

Instead, 'I'm pregnant,' popped out.

Hallie's eyes widened to the size of dinner plates. 'You're preggers? For real?'

'Oh, yeah, it's real,' Kristen said, rubbing her flat belly in a reflex action, finding it almost impossible to equate herself—the ultimate career girl—with a mother. 'The doc just told me. I had no idea.'

'Wow.'

Hallie collapsed back against the cushions, her stunned look soon replaced by the cheeky grin Kristen had grown accustomed to. 'So, who's the father? Anyone I know?'

Hallie's exaggerated, conspiratorial wink should've made Kristen laugh. Instead, dread shot through her at the thought of anyone at work finding out Nate was the father before he did.

Forcing a nonchalant tone, Kristen said, 'No.' Not a lie, exactly. The Nate she'd known for that one brief, magical night in Singapore was nothing like the Nathan Boyd, CEO that Hallie knew.

'So you're doing this on your own? That's pretty brave.'

'Actually, I have no idea what I'm going to do.'

Hallie's grin faded. 'You're going to keep it, right?'

'Uh-huh.'

Kristen's tentative response encapsulated her doubts. She'd never have contemplated any other outcome than going through with this pregnancy. But not wanting this baby had nothing to do with her lifestyle or job, and everything to do with the gut-wrenching fear which had gnawed at her since childhood; the soul-destroying fear that she'd never be a good mother because she'd never had one herself.

Being shunted from foster home to foster home had taken care of that, where the women so casually labelled 'mothers' hadn't known the first thing about caring or nurturing a child. Instead, their focus had been strictly on the dollars allocated by the government for the care of parentless kids like her, and she'd grown to hate their cold, callous indifference.

'You don't sound terribly convinced.'

Straightening, Kristen said, 'I'm having this baby.'

She might not have the foggiest idea how to be a good parent, but suddenly she knew she could do a darn sight better job than the poor excuses that had raised her.

'Fabulous!' Hallie clapped her hands like an excited two-year-old. 'I can be a surrogate aunt. Though I still think you're super-brave to be doing this alone.'

Kristen shrugged, strangely uncomfortable with an admiration she didn't deserve. 'Not really. There are tonnes of single parents out there. I'm just adding to the statistics.'

'Yeah, but a baby? Man, is that going to cramp your style.'

Hallie's eyes sparkled as she sent a pointed look at her fitted skirt and matching jacket. 'Especially your clothes style. Mind if you throw a few casts-offs my way? Your clothes are to die for.'

Kristen chuckled. Nothing fazed Hallie, even an

unexpected pregnancy, and she hoped Nate took the news as well.

'I hate to tell you, but I won't be the size of a house for long. I plan on getting back into my clothes one day.'

'Too bad.'

Hallie smiled and smothered her in a hug. 'Actually, this is cool. It's the best news I've heard in ages. Congrats, Kris. You're going to be a great mum.'

'Thanks,' Kristen mumbled after disengaging from Hallie's bear hug, gulping the rest of her water to dislodge the lump of emotion stuck in her throat, fervently hoping the tears wouldn't start again.

'You know you can count on me, right?'

Kristen nodded and made a frantic grab for a tissue out of her handbag, dabbing at her eyes before she turned on the waterworks again.

'Stop trying to make me cry,' she sniffled, while Hallie grinned and slid an arm around her shoulders.

'Okay. I'll stop. And, by the way, don't worry. Your secret's safe with me.'

'It better be. I haven't had a chance to tell Nathan yet.'

Hallie gave her a comforting squeeze. 'The boss will be fine about it. He'll hire a maternity-leave replacement for your position, and you'll be back before you can say "pooey nappy".'

'I hope you're right,' Kristen said, sending her friend a watery smile.

She had no qualms about Nate accepting the news of her impending maternity arrangements.

It was sharing the news that he was the father of her baby she had her doubts about.

'What about the dad—are you going to tell him?'

Kristen stiffened. 'I hadn't thought that far ahead,' she said, doing her best to avoid the topic.

'You know it's the right thing to do?'

Hallie's astute stare made Kristen squirm, and she shuffled back on the couch, picked up a cushion and hugged it to her tummy.

'Right?' Hallie prompted.

'Look, I've barely absorbed the news myself,' Kristen said, knowing that no amount of time would make this decision any easier.

'Well, if you don't, I think you're selfish.'

Hallie flopped back and folded her arms, her mouth a ridiculous, sulky pout.

'Tell me what you really think,' Kristen muttered, hugging the cushion tighter.

Mostly she agreed with Hallie, but this wasn't quite that straightforward.

This was Nate they were talking about. The same Nate who had erased that amazing night from his memory banks, the same Nate who had given her the cold shoulder for the last fortnight, the same Nate who was her boss.

Could she really tell him the truth?

Hallie turned to face her, a surprisingly stubborn frown firmly in place. 'Every parent has a right to know if they have a child. One of my closest friends would've given anything to know her dad, but her mum always said he was dead. Well, guess what? Turned out Dad was living around the corner the entire time, and when my friend turned up on his doorstep twenty years later he was ecstatic. Mad as hell at my friend's mum for cheating him of playing a part in her life all those years, but really chuffed he had a kid. So, unless your baby's father is an axe-murderer, which I seriously doubt, you should tell him. It's the right thing to do.'

Kristen had never seen Hallie so serious. Joking around, teasing, flippant, yes. But delivering a stern lecture like that? Uh-uh.

'You're probably right, but I just want some time to think this through, okay?'

Hallie deflated, and her trademark smile returned. 'Okay. But if you don't you know I'll be on your case, right?'

'I know.'

Kristen rolled her eyes, knowing she was lucky to have a friend like Hallie to confide in, especially considering they'd only known each other two weeks.

'Well, you've got some thinking to do, so I'll leave you to it. Ring me if you need anything.'

'Shall do.'

Kristen showed Hallie to the door and gave her an impulsive hug, before realising she didn't have any transport home.

'Hey, come back inside and I'll ring for a cab.'

'Don't worry about it. I'll catch a tram. It'll take me ten minutes to get home, max.'

'Sure?'

Hallie gave her a gentle shove back through the door. 'Go. Sit down. Think.'

'Okay, okay.' Kristen held up her hands in surrender, smiling as Hallie bounced down the path, and waved till she hit the street corner.

However, her smile faded as she closed the door and silence descended.

Sure, she might have to do a lot of thinking, but did that necessarily mean she'd come up with the right answer? The right answer for them all?

She needed time, time to adjust and figure out what to do.

CHAPTER SIX

NATE braced himself as Kris's front door creaked open and her frowning face appeared through the crack.

'Hi, how are you feeling?'

'Better.' She opened the door a fraction further, the frown intensifying as she fiddled with a chain. 'What are you doing here?'

'Sorry to drop by unannounced, but I was worried about you.'

'You don't need to be, I'm fine.'

The chain clattered against the door frame, but she didn't invite him in. Instead, she hid behind the door, only her head visible.

'Hallie said it's some kind of virus?'

'That's right.'

Her lips compressed into a thin line, and she glared at him like he'd diagnosed her with a terminal illness rather than a transient one.

So much for being concerned. He was floundering here, way out of his depth, and he'd made a major mistake dropping by.

'I'm glad you're okay. If you need more time off work, take it.'

'I'll be in first thing in the morning,' she said, her tone softening as she opened the door wider. 'Look, you may as well come in now you're here. I'm just not dressed to receive visitors, and you kind of took me by surprise showing up out of the blue like this.'

'You sure? I don't want to impose or anything.'

Her raised eyebrow told him he already had. 'You better come in before I change my mind and slam the door in your face.'

'Put like that, how can I refuse?'

He stepped into the hallway, quickly averting his gaze when he caught sight of the long, silky, purple kimono draping the gorgeous body he remembered all too well.

'The lounge is through there. Make yourself at home while I get dressed.'

He opened his mouth to protest and snapped it shut again. He didn't want her going to any trouble, especially if she was comfortable, but then having to sit across from her dressed in that sexy robe, wondering if she was naked beneath it, would make him extremely uncomfortable.

She padded up the stairs, her bare feet softly thudding against the worn boards, and he watched her for a moment, admiring the gentle swish of silk around her slim ankles and the way the material draped her toned butt, before heading for the lounge, and not up the stairs like he wanted to.

This was a bad idea.

If seeing her in those sexy suits on a daily basis was bad enough, seeing her in that flowing kimono had set his mind off on tangents he shouldn't be contemplating.

Stepping into the lounge, he did another double take.

The outside of the quaint terrace house had a homely feel to it, with its cream rendering and bottle-green fretwork but this room quickly dispelled that impression with its stark modernistic furniture, all sleek lines and devoid of colour. Beige walls, beige suede suite, and a large beige rug covering the pale floorboards, without a splash of contrasting colour or bright pictures in sight.

Another noticeable absent feature was photos. She'd told him she didn't have much family apart from two sisters, but it looked like they didn't rank highly on her scale of personal importance if their absence was any indication. He didn't have many lying around any more either, but that was because of the painful memories every time he caught an unexpected glimpse of Julia's smile, or the characteristic sparkle in her eyes he'd loved since high school.

He did a slow turn, suddenly chilled by the lifeless ambience of the room. Kris was a vibrant, outgoing woman. What was she doing, living in a place like this? A place built for families and love and warmth on the outside yet cold and indifferent on the inside. What did that say about the woman he thought he knew?

'Would you like something to drink?'

He spun around, forcing a smile to hide his discomfort. 'I'm fine, thanks.'

She hovered in the doorway, her blue eyes stark in her pale face, highlighted by the bright red of her T-shirt worn loose over dark denim jeans.

He was used to dealing with a super-confident woman strutting around the office. This waif-like Kris had him wanting to do all sorts of uncharacteristic things, like cradle her close and stroke her tousled blonde hair.

'Why don't you tell me why you're really here?'

She leaned in the doorway, hands thrust into the pockets of her jeans, her feet bare, and the fire-engine red of her painted toenails a perfect match for her T-shirt. Her pallor should've highlighted her vulnerability. However, nothing could dim the intelligence behind her direct stare, and he knew she'd settle for nothing less than the truth.

'Fine, but only if you sit down. You're making me nervous.'

Quirking a brow, she padded across the room and chose the armchair furthest from him. 'Okay, start talking.'

Rather than curling up and tucking her feet under her, like most people would in their own home, she perched on the edge of the chair as if ready for flight.

'My main reason for dropping by like this was to check up on you, but there's something else.'

'I gathered that.'

She didn't encourage him or set him at ease, her rigid posture indicative of the hands-off approach she'd adopted with him. Not that he could blame her, considering he'd been doing the same.

Sitting opposite, he leaned back on the sofa which felt as stiff as it looked. 'I owe you an apology.'

'Go on.'

He couldn't read her blank expression but the banked fire in her eyes spoke volumes. She intended to roast him over his behaviour and then make him sweat to be forgiven.

'I've been pushing you hard, much harder than anyone else at the station. And I'm having one hell of a guilt attack about the role all the extra work I've hefted on you might've played in you coming down with this bug.'

For the first time since he'd arrived, a crooked smile lit her face. 'Save your guilt. Work had nothing to do with how I'm feeling.'

He paused, staggered that one small, barely-there smile could pack such a powerful punch, slamming into his conscience with the precise hook of a prize fighter.

'Nice of you to let me off so easily, but viruses tend to strike when you're run down and I've been running you off your feet. Why don't you take tomorrow off, rest up and come back next Monday?'

She shook her head, the smile vanishing in an instant, only to be replaced by the stubborn set of lips he'd come to associate with his star executive producer. He'd seen a similar mutinous expression every time he'd brought up an idea at work she didn't agree with, every time he'd questioned her rationale.

'Thanks, but I'm fine. I'll be there bright and early tomorrow. If you ever let me get some sleep, that is.'

She cast a pointed look at her watch and he stood, wishing he could somehow make things better between them.

Sure, he didn't want to get too close, but he'd be damned if they continued in this cold manner.

'I miss the easygoing rapport we had in Singapore,' he said, holding out his hand to help her off the chair, knowing he shouldn't have brought up the night they'd sworn to forget but unable to stop.

He needed to do something to shock her out of the casual indifference shrouding her like armour.

He expected her to ignore his outstretched hand, but

yet again she surprised him, placing her hand in his and allowing him to pull her to her feet.

'I do too,' she said, so softly he had to lean forward to catch her words—which would've been fine if it hadn't brought him scant inches away from her lush mouth, and close enough to smell her faint rose essence, subtle and enticing as a stroll through a rose garden on a warm summer's day.

She stared at him, her blue eyes wide with uncertainty and his heart clenched at the vulnerability behind the tough-girl exterior.

For all her attitude Kris reached out to him on a deeper level, and if he wasn't careful he'd find himself sucked into a vortex of emotion he didn't want.

'Friends?'

He squeezed her hand, wishing he could raise it to his lips and kiss it, wishing he could hold it for ever.

But he wasn't a 'for ever' type of guy, not any more.

The vulnerability in her eyes quickly faded, replaced by her usual tough veneer, and she pulled her hand out of his. 'Friends it is.'

She headed for the hallway and he had no option but to follow, trailing after her like some teenager with a crush.

'Remember, if you need extra time off—'

'See you tomorrow,' she said, holding open the door and scuffing her foot impatiently on the floor.

'Righto.'

He brushed past her, knowing his visit hadn't achieved much more than make a start in broaching the yawning gap between them.

She hadn't bought his false apology.

He'd wanted to apologise for pushing her away, for treating her like a stranger rather than the woman who had woken him out of a three-year stupor, but he'd baulked at the last minute, covering it up by referring to work.

So he wasn't ready to bare his soul.

He'd reached out to her, hadn't he? By referring to their night of passion and the connection they'd shared he'd virtually admitted he hadn't forgotten it. Nor did he want to, and in finally admitting it maybe he could get beyond this obsession gripping him for the woman standing in front of him looking ready to boot him down the front path.

'Was there something else?'

'Actually, there was.'

He paused, searching for the right words, knowing he had to make up for the way he'd treated her. 'You're a smart woman. I guess you've realised I haven't only been pushing you hard, I've been behaving like a bastard as well.'

'Well, I wouldn't put it that strongly,' she said, the corners of her mouth twitching and drawing his attention to the fullness of her lips, those same lips which had prompted him to lose his mind that balmy night in Singapore.

'It's true. And we both know it. I'd just like to say it's going to stop.'

Her lips curved into a full-fledged grin, alleviating some of the tired lines tugging around her mouth. 'About time. Though if I'd known the results a quick-fire faint would produce, I would've tried it last week.'

He grimaced. 'Was I really that bad?'

'Worse!'

Shadows flickered across her eyes, her frailty urging him to sweep her into his arms and never let go.

'I'm sorry,' he murmured, reaching up to cup her cheek, unable to stop himself from touching her, from reassuring her that he'd be doing things differently from now on.

'No worries,' she said, her wide-eyed blue gaze locked on his as she moved her cheek an infinitesimal millimetre and leaned into his hand.

Powerless to resist the urge he'd had since he'd first laid eyes on her tonight, he broached the gap between them, slid his hand around to cradle her head, and lowered his mouth to hers.

She sighed as his lips grazed hers, soft, coaxing, in the barest of kisses. However, he should've known that a gentle kiss wouldn't be enough, not nearly enough with this incredible woman, and the moment she angled her head slightly was the moment he lost it.

Wrapping his arms around her, he pulled her flush against him, relishing their perfect fit as his mouth re-captured hers, deepening the kiss till he could barely breathe for wanting her.

Desire slammed through his body, sending his mind into meltdown as he kissed her with all the pent-up passion which had been steadily building since she'd re-entered his life.

A crazy, fiery, no-holds-barred kiss, sending his libido into orbit and their working relationship up in flames.

Suddenly, Kris braced her hands on his chest and pushed him away, her breathing ragged and her eyes flashing fire.

'That wasn't very professional,' she said, her voice deliberately cool, and in stark contrast to her flushed cheeks.

'No, I guess not.'

Unable to keep a satisfied grin off his face, he turned away from her confused stare and strode down the concrete path away from temptation.

CHAPTER SEVEN

'It's fantastic!'

Kristen turned to Nate and struggled not to fling her arms around his neck as her gaze reluctantly left the TV screen and focussed on the man who had backed her one hundred percent on this exciting project.

Nate tried a mock frown and failed, his answering grin setting her heart thudding. 'Hmm…I'm not sure. Could do with a bit of work.'

'Are you serious?'

She leaped up from her chair and stalked across the conference room, filling a cup with water and wondering when she'd last felt this energised, this alive.

'No, I'm not serious.'

He chuckled and she swivelled to face him, hand on hip. 'Joke all you like, but we both know what we've just seen is going to take Australian TV by storm.'

'That's what I like to see. Confidence.'

He joined her at the water cooler, invading her personal space with his presence, standing so close her body warmed from the heat radiating off his, and she took a subtle step back, needing to re-establish some distance between them.

Exuberance over success in the workplace was one thing; jumping her boss because she couldn't get the memory of that unexpected, scintillating kiss on her doorstep a week ago off her mind was another.

'Tell me it's not the best travel show you've ever seen.'

He drained his water and lobbed the cup in the bin, before turning to face her, the excitement in his eyes a dead giveaway for what he was thinking before he opened his mouth to respond.

'Honestly? It's some of the best work I've ever seen. You've done an incredible job, Kris.'

He touched her arm, an all-too-brief squeeze designed to convey his pleasure in her work, but predictably her pulse raced and her mind took flight, resurrecting the many ways he'd touched her all those months ago on that one special night.

'Thanks.'

She headed back to the table and started gathering up her portfolio, knowing she needed to escape as soon as possible. In her current buoyant mood, spending one second longer with Nate could prove disastrous.

Along with her fertile imagination she had a distinct case of pregnancy hormones sending her libido crazy, and with a sexy guy like Nate around it was becoming increasingly harder to think of him in boss-terms only.

'You know this means I'm going to expect this standard from you all the time, right?'

She jumped, his voice coming from way too close over her right shoulder, and she shovelled documents faster. 'No problems. At least I know if I keep producing work of this standard you'll be nice to me.'

Oops! She hadn't meant to say the last bit, even if she

thought it was the truth. Ever since that unexpected kiss he'd changed for the better in the workplace, and they'd grown closer, developing a strong working bond which was fast moving towards friendship.

She'd attributed his change to her performance, but maybe there was something more behind the turnaround.

'I've already apologised for my earlier behaviour,' he said, reaching out and taking hold of her arm before slowly turning her around to face him.

Determined not to let him see how he affected her, she tilted her chin up and hoped her expression wouldn't give away her turbulent emotions: fear he'd revert back to being cold, fear of this new and improved Nate, but most of all fear of how easily she could fall for him given half a chance.

'I know, I remember.'

How could she forget? She'd been ready to deck him that night on her doorstep; he'd kissed her senseless, undermining all her defences in one swift, scorching kiss.

Something akin to desire flickered in his eyes before he dropped his hands and turned away, intent on stuffing documents into his briefcase.

'Good. In that case, you know I meant what I said. That's all in the past. We're a great team, and I intend for us to have a long and profitable relationship.'

His matter-of-fact tone snapped her out of the sensual fog enveloping her brain as she stilled her hands before they could rub the exact spots he'd touched her a moment ago.

Nate was her boss. She was his star employee. They had a 'long and *profitable* relationship' ahead of them.

That's all she was to him, a great worker. It was all

she'd ever be, and no matter how much she analysed that kiss it had obviously been an aberration, a spur-of-the-moment apology from a guy feeling bad about how he'd treated her.

Nothing more.

'Right. See you tomorrow,' she said, shrugging into her jacket, its tight fit reminding her of something else that would potentially bind them in a relationship, though this time it would have nothing to do with work.

She still hadn't made up her mind about telling Nate about the baby though the closer they grew, work or not, she knew the time was fast approaching where she had to make a decision one way or the other.

'I'm really thrilled this is working out, Kris.'

He finally straightened and glanced at her, an inscrutable expression in his dark-chocolate eyes, and for a moment an irrational spark of hope flared to life that maybe, just maybe, he was referring to something other than work.

'Me too.'

Forcing a cheery smile, she waved and sailed out the door, silently praying he had no idea of the giant crush she'd developed.

'Oh, my.'

Kristen stared at the big, flat LCD screen in the corner while the doctor moved a detector over her stomach, skidding through the cold gel as he moved it every which way, showing her in startling clarity that she was pregnant.

'The bub is a perfect size for fourteen weeks,' the doctor said, whose name she'd forgotten the instant she'd stepped into the room, her scared gaze riveted to the monitors and screens crowding the single bed in a makeshift cubicle in his office. 'I'll just take a few more measurements and we'll be done here.'

She nodded, barely aware of anything bar the tiny baby on the screen, its knees tucked up to its chest, cosy and secure with not a care in the world, while her heart raced and her palms grew damp with the enormity of what she was doing.

That little, defenceless baby was hers, from its ten tiny, perfectly formed fingers to its miniature toes. Tears stung her eyes and she blinked rapidly, unwilling to blubber in front of a stranger. Time enough for that at the birth.

As her eyes stayed riveted to the screen the baby's hand moved towards its face as if waving, and Kristen's heart clenched with a surge of instinctual love. In that moment, the fact this pregnancy was real hit her in a tidal wave of emotion, leaving her breathless with joy, fear and anticipation.

'Almost there,' the doctor said, taking snapshots of the baby by hitting a few keys on the elaborate keyboard linked to a monitor.

She wanted to say *take all the time in the world*, because for this one significant moment in time she realised something. Coming face to face with her baby, seeing the hard evidence she was carrying a real, live little person inside of her, hammered home the enormity of the situation.

She hadn't created this tiny miracle all by herself. And, as much as she'd prevaricated over the dilemma of whether to tell Nate or not, seeing the living, breathing evidence of the life they'd created left her with no choice.

She had to tell him.

It was the right thing to do.

Though now she'd made the decision her stomach somersaulted at the thought.

Since the night he'd dropped by her place a fortnight ago they'd forged a strong working relationship. He'd let go of whatever hang-up he'd had the first two weeks and they had become closer than she'd dared hope, considering their capricious start. Not that they were best buddies or anything, but it was nice to consider the boss a friend rather than an enemy.

However, how friendly would he be when she dumped her pregnancy surprise on him?

Most guys would run a mile. Then again, Nate wasn't most guys.

For a CEO who owned a substantial percentage of Australia's entertainment interests, he didn't have a mean bone in his body and, though he hadn't shaken the inherent sadness which seemed to be a part of him, he smiled most days, a smile which lit up her world if she were completely honest.

'All done.' The doctor wiped the gel off her tummy and handed her a small picture. 'Here. One for your album.'

Grinning like an idiot, she traced the baby's outline with a fingertip, unprepared for the surge of fierce, intense love which arrowed through her body and lodged directly in her heart.

Though she didn't have a clue about parenting, she would be the best mother if it killed her. She'd buy a library full of books, take parenting classes, do whatever it took to ensure her baby had the best mum in the world.

'Thanks,' she murmured, raising tear-filled eyes to see the young doctor smiling at her.

'Really hits home right about now, huh?'

She nodded, clutching the small photo like Charlie holding onto the golden ticket to the chocolate factory.

'Make sure you schedule another ultrasound for twenty weeks on your way out,' he said, helping her down from the table. 'I'll see you then.'

'Okay.'

Placing the photo on the bed, Kristen zipped up her trousers and slipped her stockinged feet into stiletto pumps, her gaze never leaving the first picture of her child.

Her child?

Sighing, she picked up the picture and slid it into her handbag. *Their* child. Nate was the father, and he deserved to know no matter how protective she might feel towards her unborn baby.

Whether he wanted anything to do with the baby or not, it should be his decision to make, not hers.

This baby was real.

This baby was theirs.

Suddenly, Kristen knew it was time to give Nate the news. This wasn't only about her, and a good mother always put her child's needs first.

Starting now.

Kristen opened the door to her dinner guest, her breath catching as she caught sight of Nate standing on her doorstep wearing dark denim, a navy designer T-shirt and a smile.

The guy was seriously gorgeous, and she could easily fall for him given half a chance.

But that was out of the question. She had a baby to care for, a life to build for them both, and her needs would come a far second to that of her child.

'These are for you.'

He handed her five large blocks of Swiss chocolate with the gooiest fudge-caramel centres, her favourite, and she welcomed him in.

'How did you know?'

'I've seen you devouring the odd block or two at your desk.'

The odd block or two? She reckoned she'd bought out the local chocolatier with her intense cravings for the creamy, smooth chocolate that melted on her tongue. So her baby would have a sweet tooth. If that was the worst trait he or she inherited from its mother, she'd be lucky.

'Have you been spying on me?'

He grinned. 'Of course. I always keep an eye on my best exec producers. James Bond has nothing on me.'

'You could give James a run for his money,' she said, ushering him into the cosy dining room set for two and handing him a bottle opener. 'In the successful stakes, of course.'

Uh-oh, had she actually said that, the bit about him giving James Bond a run for his money? Going by his cocky smile she had, and he probably knew exactly how she was comparing him—in the sexiness stakes. Her cover-up for her gaff had been pathetic at best.

She bustled about the table, handing him the wine to uncork while she topped up her glass with sparkling mineral water.

'Wine?'

'No thanks,' she said, the mere fumes sending a wave of nausea crashing over her.

She hadn't been too bad with morning sickness, but

come six p.m. her hormones surged, and the faintest of smells set her off and running for the loo.

Indicating he take a seat, she slid into the chair opposite. 'I'm not having wine, though I thought you might like some. It's the one you ordered in Singapore, your favourite, I believe.'

'You remembered?'

His expression relaxed as he sat down, though the wariness never left his eyes. He had no idea what he was doing here, and it was time she enlightened him.

'Uh-huh,' she said, barely refraining from adding *how could I forget anything about that evening?*

He poured himself a glass of wine, his steady stare never leaving her for an instant.

'I must say, this dinner invitation came as a pleasant surprise.'

She almost choked on her mineral water. Not half as much a surprise as it would be before the evening ended.

Replacing her glass on the table for fear of sloshing the lot, she clasped her hands to stop from fiddling, and looked him straight in the eye.

'I wanted us to have some quiet time together away from the office.'

'Really?'

She couldn't fathom the expression in his eyes. Confusion? Interest? Fear?

Nodding, she said, 'I have something to tell you, and it's important.'

Curiosity replaced confusion in his coal-dark eyes, and he leaned forward, all his attention focussed on her.

'Go ahead, shoot. Though, if you're gunning for a raise, forget it.'

Her nervous laugh sounded hollow. 'I'm pregnant and you're the father,' she blurted, horrified at the inane way the words flew out of her mouth, grateful he finally knew the truth.

The smile died on his lips as he stared at her, blanching, his pallor matching the sickly beige of the walls.

'What?'

'I thought the chocolate gorging might've been a dead giveaway?'

Her false bravado petered out quickly as he didn't move a muscle, stunned into immovability, staring at her in wide-eyed shock.

'But we used protection.'

'Condoms are only ninety-seven percent effective,' she said, watching him compute the figures, but the information not really sinking in. 'I know this must be pretty shocking for you. I felt the same way when I found out—'

'How long have you known?'

She looked away, pretending to study the elaborate table setting. 'Since that day I fainted.'

'And you've waited till now to tell me?'

She wouldn't have been surprised if he'd exploded or lost his temper or jumped up from the table. Instead, his cold, icy control terrified her more than any of the reactions she'd anticipated.

Reaching a hand across the table to comfort him, she flinched as he leaned away from her and out of reach.

'I wasn't sure if I wanted to tell you or not. It was a big decision to make, so I wanted to take my time, think about it and make sure I made the right one.'

If he'd been pale before, he turned positively ghostly now.

'And have you? Made the right decision, I mean? After all, it must've been real tough working out if you think I'm the kind of guy who can handle being told he's about to become a father.'

He pushed away from the table so fast his chair slammed onto the floor, fury etched into every tense line of his body.

She shook her head, hating how this was going. She should have led up to the news, broken it to him gently, tried to formulate some answers to the inevitable questions he would have.

Instead, she'd spilled the news quicker than she'd dropped her guard around him that night in Singapore.

Hating the surge of tears at the mess she'd made of everything, she said, 'Look, Nate, it wasn't like that. It took me a while to absorb the news. I just wanted to make sure I was doing the right thing in telling you.'

Clenching his fists, he turned to face her, his frigid glare freezing her heart.

'You should've told me earlier.'

'Maybe,' she said, sipping at her mineral water in an effort to buy some time, to give him an opportunity to calm down.

Not that she could blame him for reacting like this. She'd bawled, he'd ranted. Everyone handled life-changing news in their own way and, boy, was his life in for a major change if he wanted to be a part of their child's life.

'But I can't turn back time or change the way I've gone about this, Nate. Believe me, I've really thought about this long and hard, and once I'd made the decision I really wanted you to know.'

He grunted, fixed her with another icy glare, before shaking his head, righting his chair and sitting back down.

'The baby's doing fine, by the way,' she said, hoping to focus his attention on the real issue here—their child—and away from how much he'd like to throttle her.

His hand shook as he reached for his wine, and he quickly took a healthy swig before replacing the glass and dropping his hand out of sight, as if embarrassed by a physical sign of his obvious shock.

'That's good. And how are you?'

'Okay, apart from the usual stuff like morning sickness.'

'How far along are you?'

'About fourteen weeks.'

His gaze flickered to her belly, strategically disguised behind a loose, flowing peasant top.

'You can't tell.'

'I'm not that big yet,' she said, grateful they'd moved onto discussing the baby and away from his rage, but wishing they could fall back into their natural camaraderie rather than speaking in these stilted syllables.

'A baby,' he muttered, draining half his glass of wine before shaking his head.

They lapsed into silence, his eyes round, dark orbs in his pale face, stark in their bleak expression, her gaze darting to his to ascertain the slightest change in mood.

After thirty tension-fraught seconds which felt like a lifetime, she knew she had to get the rest out before she bolted upstairs and let the waterworks flow.

'I told you because I believe you have a right to

know, not because I expect anything from you. Whether you want to be involved or not is entirely up to you…' She trailed off, horrified by the pain which jagged across his face, his striking features almost collapsing into a crumpled heap.

'I don't believe this,' he muttered, running a hand over his face, rubbing his eyes as if trying to erase the memory of the last few minutes—maybe erasing the memory of the night that had landed them in this parenting role together.

You better believe it! she wanted to scream.

In fact, in the face of his reaction, she wanted to jump up and down and throw a tantrum to end all tantrums.

She'd worked so hard to stay calm, to tell him in the right way, to understand the roller-coaster of emotion he'd just stepped onto, but as he raised stricken eyes to her she wanted to shout, wave her arms about, do anything to snap him out of it.

Struggling to keep her voice steady, she said, 'What part don't you believe? The part about being a father, being involved or the role you played in all of this?'

Some of her anger must've been audible, because he sat back and folded his arms, pinning her with a stare that could turn her to stone.

'Don't patronise me,' he snapped, his lips compressed in a thin, rigid line. 'I'm well aware of my *role* in all of this. As for being involved, what do you want me to say?'

Suddenly, the fragile hold on her temper broke. 'Tell me what you're thinking. Tell me how you're feeling. Tell me what I can do to make this easier. Tell me whatever you damn well please, but for God's sake stop blaming me for something that isn't my fault!'

She thought he'd really lose it then, but her tirade had an unexpected effect, as his shoulders softened and he reached across the table as if to take her hand before thinking better of it.

'This isn't your fault.'

'Damn right it's not,' she muttered, downing the rest of her mineral water and topping up, anything to keep her hands busy and away from strangling him, or touching him, whichever was worse.

'I can't tell you what you want to hear because I have no idea what I'm feeling, let alone what I'm going to do about any of this.'

She heard the sincerity in his voice but it didn't make this any easier. The man she'd hoped would stand up and be counted the moment he found out about his unborn baby wasn't feeding her the reassuring lines she'd wanted to hear.

Sighing, she pushed away from the table.

'Look, I know this is a big deal, and I'm well aware you probably need some time to absorb what I've just told you. Why don't we skip dinner?'

Gratitude flickered through his eyes, the first sign of any emotion other than shock or pain.

'You sure?'

Hating the way her heart sank at his first instinct to bolt, she nodded.

'Go ahead. If you want to talk some more, you know where to find me.'

With as much dignity as she could muster, Kris headed up the stairs. She needed to get away to process her disappointment, to rationalise the disillusionment that, despite the faint hope that Nate would be as thrilled as she was about this baby, he wasn't.

It didn't surprise her, yet she couldn't help the wave of sadness which washed over her as she realised what a delusional fool she'd been for hoping her wretched crush could morph into something more, something they could build on and strengthen in time for the baby's arrival.

Blinking against the tears burning her eyes, she padded up the stairs, hating the finality of the front door slamming as Nate left.

Nate staggered from Kris's house like a drunk, the half glass of wine he'd had sloshing around his stomach till he thought he'd throw up.

Kris was pregnant.

He was the father.

Straightening, he glanced back at the house, his heart clenching at the sight of the woman carrying his child silhouetted against an upstairs window before she quickly closed the blinds.

He'd known something was different lately.

She'd been too withdrawn, too accepting of his proposals the last couple of weeks, agreeing to practically everything he'd put forward without so much as a minor skirmish or argument.

He'd attributed it to their new-found truce, and in a way he'd been too happy to question it. Building a strong working relationship with her had been rewarding, fostering a friendship even more so.

He loved the way they were on the same wavelength. He'd have an idea, she'd put the finishing touches on it.

He'd propose an amendment, she'd sanction it. They were a great team, and he could envisage RX moving forward into the upper echelon of Australian TV at a rate of knots.

But it was more than that.

He loved her quicksilver smile, the triumph in her deep blue eyes when they made an idea happen, her loud laugh when RX's latest comedy series hit the top of the ratings. He loved her fierce independence, and now all that was about to change, courtesy of him.

She was carrying *his* child.

Hell.

Bracing himself against the front fence, he took a deep breath, the crisp, bracing Melbourne air filling his lungs, hopefully clearing his head.

He couldn't do this.

No matter how much he liked Kris, he couldn't be the man she wanted.

Taking a chance on fatherhood was a risk he wasn't willing to take.

Releasing the fence, he turned away from her house and strode down the street towards his car, his long, angry steps eating up the pavement.

If hearing Kris's news had shocked him, it had nothing on the bolt of disappointment when he'd realised he couldn't be the father she wanted for her child—yet for one brief, crazy moment when she'd first told him he'd had a startling vision of the two of them together, his arm around her while she cradled their baby.

Irrational, stupid and beyond belief, the absurd surge of hope that their one incredible night together could've resulted in a baby had thrilled him before he'd bolted, running from his demons.

He didn't want to be a father.

Reaching his car, he slammed a hand against the bonnet, hating the painful memories slashing through the fog of confusion caused by Kris's revelation.

Could he take a risk again?

No, he couldn't do it.

With his head pounding with unanswered questions, Nate gunned the engine and slid away from the kerb.

He needed time to think, time to get his head around the fact he'd fathered a child, and what on earth he was going to do about it.

CHAPTER EIGHT

'YOU wanted to see me?'

Nate nodded and beckoned Kristen in, scribbling furiously on a notepad while he mumbled a string of 'uh-huhs' into the phone squeezed between his ear and shoulder.

She stepped into his office, wishing she had the guts to quit. It had crossed her mind several times since he'd left her place two nights ago. It would be so difficult to work with him, seeing him on a daily basis, trying to pretend that everything was okay, when as a matter of fact she wanted to clobber him over the head for being a cold, callous cretin.

And she'd thought her string of lousy foster mothers had been bad!

At least they'd feigned interest in her at the start, whereas Nate didn't seem interested in his son or daughter at all.

He hadn't tried to contact her, hadn't phoned or visited when she'd called in sick to work yesterday. Nothing, and his silence spoke volumes.

Some people were cut out to be parents and some weren't, and till a few months ago she'd fallen into the latter category herself. But that was before she'd woken up and smelt the ginger tea—a godsend for her nausea. In a way she should be grateful he'd shown his true colours now and hadn't strung her child along, promising birthday visits and ponies only to renege on every vow at the last minute.

She'd hated the false promises more than the lack of affection from her numerous foster parents, and she'd be damned if she sat back and let her child go through the same heartache.

Cupping his hand over the mouthpiece, he murmured, 'Sorry, this will only take a minute.'

She nodded, not caring if he took an eternity on the phone and never spoke to her again.

Being here, sitting across from him like nothing had happened, grated. She couldn't quit no matter how much she wanted to. She'd made a vow to be the best mum she could, and for her that meant staying at home for the baby's first year at least, which meant she needed to scrounge and save every penny she could now. Besides, who would employ a pregnant woman for the next few months only?

She had no choice.

She had to act the model employee, while eyeing the steel letter-opener within arm's reach and imagining creative ways she could make her heartless boss squirm.

Hanging up the phone, Nate threw down his pen and said, 'Sorry about that. Interstate conference-call took longer than expected.'

She ignored his apology, eager to get straight to the point. The less they saw of each other, business arena or not, the better.

'What did you want to see me about?'

'This.'

He handed her a gilt-edged embossed invitation and she opened it, scanning over the words with little interest. 'An invitation to the Logies. So?'

'We're going.'

The stiff cardboard invitation to the Australian television awards crumpled in her clenched fist like tissue paper, and she forced herself to relax.

'You might be. I'm not.'

It took every ounce of willpower to place the balled invitation on the desk and not throw it in his face. Now, if she could manage to hold onto her temper for the few steps between the desk and the door, she'd be doing well indeed.

'Actually, we both have to go. Una and Alan are both interstate this weekend, so that leaves us to represent the station.'

'Take someone else,' she said, shifting her weight from foot to foot, enjoying standing over him, but hating the way the straps on her stilettos cut into her ankles.

Maybe it was time to forego fashion for comfort now that she was retaining a bit of fluid. The joys of motherhood…and this was only the start!

He shook his head, reaching for the invitation and smoothing it out.

'No can do. We're the head honchos of RX at the moment, we have to attend. It wouldn't look good if we didn't go, not to mention giving the rumour-mill fodder for the next few months. You know we're launching an all-out attack on the ratings soon. For the sake of good PR we have to be there, no excuses.'

Kristen mustered her worst intimidating glare, knowing she had no choice but to go along to television's biggest awards night—with him!

Damn him for being right.

Damn him for putting her in this predicament.

Most of all, damn him for eliciting the faintest thrill of pleasure at the thought of accompanying him, especially when she was supposed to be hating him right now.

'Fine. E-mail me the details and I'll meet you there.'

She turned on her heel and headed for the door without a backward glance.

'Kris?'

She bit her tongue to keep from responding and kept moving. Only a few more steps…

'We need to talk about the baby.'

She stopped dead, swivelling so fast her head spun. 'Now?'

'I didn't want to have this conversation here,' he muttered, running a hand over his eyes as if to obliterate a host of memories. She knew the feeling. 'Poor form on my part, but I can't let this wait till later. I don't know about you, but I can't function with the two of us like this.'

'We're professionals, Nate,' she said, wondering if he remembered using similar words on her first day when he'd belittled what they'd shared in Singapore, negating it to nothing with his nonchalance. 'We need to function as best we can regardless of our personal situations.'

'I deserved that, but can we talk?'

He crossed the space between them in a flash, gripping her upper arms so she couldn't move, and darn if her pulse didn't leap and jump and thud all over the place.

Stupid pregnancy hormones.

Trying to ignore the warmth seeping into her body from his touch, she said, 'Do you really want to talk about the baby here? Now? That's what the other night was about, you know. If you hadn't run scared, that is.'

His dark eyes widened, and all colour drained from his face as his grip on her arms tightened, his fingers biting into her tender flesh till she squirmed.

'You don't know anything about me.'

Yanking free of his grasp, she sent him a scathing look. 'Too right I don't. Funny thing is, I thought I did. I never thought you'd be the type of guy to turn tail and run and then give me the cold shoulder when you finally see me again.'

'You're right, I'm sorry…' He trailed off, rubbing the bridge of his nose as if he had a thumper of a headache, closing his eyes for a second before they snapped open and fixed her with a stare that could have frozen nitrogen. 'My reaction has nothing to do with you.'

Raising an eyebrow, she tried to match his cold stare and failed. She couldn't do it when she glimpsed the devastation behind the forced coolness in his eyes, and wondered what or who had put it there.

'You're wrong. It has everything to do with me. We're in this together.'

She reached out and gripped his hand, giving it a quick squeeze before letting go. Touching him, even for something as innocuous as a comforting squeeze on the hand, felt way too good. 'If you want to be, that is.'

Shaking his head, he perched his butt on the back of the chair, his steady stare never leaving her face. 'Honestly? I don't know what I want right now.'

'Oh.'

'I know this is hard for you, but I need some more time,' he said, his grave expression imploring her to understand something she had no idea about as she wondered how her life had got so complicated.

A few months ago the hardest decision she'd had to make was which suit to wear to work, and now, thanks to one amazing night, they'd woven an intricate web of parenthood which had them both confused and scared.

'Time. Right.'

She nodded, hating how high and tight and squeaky her voice sounded, hating the threat of tears prickling the back of her eyelids more.

'Hey, it's okay,' he said, enveloping her in a hug before she knew what was happening, and though her first instinct was to pull away she ignored it, relaxing into his embrace, wondering when she'd last been held like this, comforted like this.

Probably that night in Singapore, when the same man had wrapped his arms around her, though back then there had been nothing but passion and heat and an overwhelming attraction.

Her skin tingled at the scorching recollection, and she placed her hands on his chest and pushed away, albeit reluctantly.

She needed to get out of here before she blubbered. Being held by Nate, enveloped by his purely masculine scent, cradled in his strong arms, did nothing but short-circuit her brain and make her forget every logical reason she had for pushing him away.

'It's okay to be scared, you know,' she said, knowing most guys would be blown away by news of impending fatherhood, yet unable to shake the feeling there was more behind Nate's reaction than simple fear.

He wavered between anger, coldness, fear and warmth, vacillating all over the place when he was usually so commanding and in control.

'Scared? I'm terrified,' he said, the serious expression on his face telling her far more than his honest words did.

There *was* something more at play here, but she couldn't push him. If he hadn't made a decision about being involved with the baby yet, what right did she have to push him for answers to questions she could barely formulate?

'Hey, I'm scared too. I know it's a big deal, and besides, I've had longer to absorb it all than you have.'

Cupping her cheek, he brushed his thumb along her skin, sending shivers skittering through her body. 'Thanks for being so understanding.'

'Yeah, that's me.'

She stilled under his touch, her breath catching as his thumb rasped across her cheek for a brief moment before dropping away. 'I don't even know if you like babies.'

Some guys did, some would run a mile at the barest hint of a goo-goo or ga-ga, and she'd wondered where Nate stood ever since she'd discovered the pregnancy.

He sighed and looked away, and her heart plummeted. From the moment Nate had said he wanted to talk about the baby, she'd built an elaborate fantasy in her head, one where Nate loved the baby and grew to feel half of what she felt for him, wrapping them all up in one neat family package.

However, with his crestfallen expression and guilty gaze, he'd ripped the bow off in a swift, painful action, exposing her fantasy for what it was: an empty dream without all the trimmings.

'It's complicated,' he said, finally raising his eyes to meet hers again.

'Right now, complication is my middle name,' she said, forcing a brittle, hollow laugh which echoed eerily around the room.

'Look, I want to explain it to you, but I can't get into it right now. This isn't the time or place.'

'Maybe later?'

Her voice came out soft, small, shy, like a coy teen-ager asking a boy out on a date, and she felt just as un-certain and gauche, hanging on his answer with hope in her heart.

His face fell along with her hopes. 'I can't. I'm flying to Brisbane in a few hours to one of the other divisions. I'll be there all week, getting back late Sunday afternoon before the Logies.'

'Oh.'

Could this get any more convoluted?

Maybe she and Nate weren't meant to sort things out. Maybe she'd be better off pinning her hopes on winning the lottery?

A million-to-one chance, about the same odds she had as ever getting on the same page as Nate.

'Hey, I promise we'll talk after the Logies, okay?'

He tipped her chin up, his gaze warm and steady, im-ploring her to trust him.

Like she knew anything about trust.

She'd had her scant personal belongings stolen by the foster family's own kids at the first foster home she'd been dumped in, she'd been let down at parent-teacher interviews by her second foster mum on no less than three occasions, and the third, fourth and fifth foster homes she'd lived in had been rife with verbal and psychological abuse.

What she knew about trust equalled what she knew about babies—next to nothing.

'I don't expect anything of you,' she said, stepping away, glad to re-establish some control over her personal space, hating the bereft feeling when his arms fell to his sides. 'You know that's not what the other night was about. I just thought you had a right to know.'

'Thanks. It means a lot.'

However, he didn't look grateful. In fact, he looked downright uncomfortable, as if being a dad was the last thing he wanted.

Well, she'd make it easy for him.

'No one needs to know about this,' she said, fiddling with the edging of her jacket. 'I won't name you as the father on the birth certificate.'

She'd thought she was doing him a favour.

By the angry crimson flush creeping up his neck, and his thin, compressed lips, she'd thought wrong.

'I'm not ashamed of this child or being recognised as the father. I just need some time.'

Time for what?

Time to invent excuses why he couldn't be around?

Time to make himself scarce?

She could've asked him, but she wouldn't give him the satisfaction of knowing how much his answers meant to her.

For some strange reason, it suddenly mattered why he needed time. A lot.

After the other night she'd resigned herself to being her baby's sole parent, yet now having Nate take responsibility seemed paramount.

She wanted to know what was driving him, what was behind the fleeting guilt she glimpsed at times. Because maybe, just maybe, if she understood more about what motivated him, she'd have a chance of making him see how great being a parent to their child could be.

With her thoughts swinging as wildly as her emotions, courtesy of her hormones, she knew she'd better leave before she did something crazy—like fling herself back into his comforting arms.

'More time? Sure. We're not going anywhere.'

She patted her tummy, a never-ending sense of awe flooding her body at the bump already there, while his panicked glance flickered between her belly and her face.

Whoa! How could a capable, take-charge CEO look like he was about to faint at the thought of being a father? Maybe he wasn't half the man she'd thought he was.

And maybe you need to give the guy a break.

He'd said he would explain on Sunday and she had to give him the benefit of the doubt. She had no other option.

'I'll pick you up at seven?'

'Fine,' she said, wondering how she'd get through the rest of the week knowing that they would be discussing their baby's future after some silly, flash awards-night. 'See you then.'

She spun on her heel and opened the door, needing some air, needing some distance between her and the man who made her dream and want and crave things she had no right believing in.

'Kris?'

'Yeah?'

She glanced over her shoulder, unable to fathom the intense expression casting shadows over his handsome face.

'Thanks for giving me a chance.'

Flashing him a wan smile, she headed out of his office, wondering if he meant a chance at being a father, a chance at explaining, or something else entirely.

CHAPTER NINE

THE brass knocker clanged noisily against Kristen's front door, and she slipped on her shoes, grabbed her evening bag and made a mad dash for the stairs, forcing herself to slow when she reached the top.

'Sorry about the bumpy ride,' she murmured, caressing her belly as she descended the stairs to greet Nate, filled with uncertainty and fear and longing, the latter a terrible, desperate yearning for a man she knew could never be hers.

For if Nate hadn't wanted her before she was pregnant there was no way she'd fall for any sudden change of heart.

She wouldn't put it past an upstanding guy like him to want to do the right thing and include her in his grand plans for giving his child the perfect life—if he wanted an involvement with his child, that was.

Pity he hadn't realised they could've had the perfect life before the baby had obligated him to her.

Opening the door with a welcoming smile, she said, 'Hi, you're back.'

Not the most scintillating line, but not bad considering her mind had shut down the second she'd caught sight of Nate in a designer tuxedo, his dark eyes sparkling, a sexy smile playing about his mouth, and his hands filled with a giant box covered in adorable teddy bears.

'You look beautiful,' he said, the banked heat of his top-to-toe glance setting her body alight, his admiration thrilling her. She'd spent an inordinate amount of time with her make-up, hair and adjusting the exquisite A-line empire-style dress of mauve chiffon, gathered over her nicely expanding bust and falling in loose folds to her ankles.

She wanted Nate to see her as an attractive woman.

She wanted him to see her as more than the mother of his child.

Stupid, foolish, crazy?

Definitely but she couldn't help but wish her baby would have more than she'd ever had—a father to protect her, to give her advice, to beat off randy teenagers like those who'd treated her as trash because she'd had no parents and no one who particularly cared.

Not that she was completely delusional. She didn't expect Nate and her to be a couple, but she wanted them to establish a bond, a close friendship which would envelop her baby in love and security. Two things she would've given anything for growing up.

'And this is for you.'

'Thanks, come in.'

She stepped aside, inhaling deeply as he brushed past her, the heady scent of his signature aftershave sending her receptors into meltdown. She'd never forget that smell, its tangy freshness a lingering reminder of the incredible night they'd shared and the way his skin had pressed up against hers in so many delightful ways, branding her own with his exotic scent.

'Aren't you going to open it?'

He laid the box down on the dining table and she nodded, suddenly shy at the way he devoured her with his eyes, the glint of desire she glimpsed there a potent reminder of what they'd shared, what they could share again if he threw caution to the wind and she lost her mind.

I'll blame the hormones again, she thought, remembering how she'd swiftly flipped past the chapter in one of the books where it had stated that expectant mothers often found their libidos out of control.

That had to be true considering all she could think of right at this minute was ripping that stuffy bow-tie off Nate's neck, tearing open his snowy-white shirt and burying her face against his amazing rock-hard chest.

'Kris?'

Heat flushed her cheeks—she could easily have skipped the blush—and she opened the box, her heart expanding with emotion as she lifted out a giant, purple hippo wearing a goofy smile.

'He's gorgeous,' she said, blinking back sudden tears at Nate's generosity, hoping this was the sign she'd hoped for, the sign that he wanted to be a part of their child's life and, if so, knowing this would be the first of many presents for their lucky child.

'There's something in there for you too,' he said, gently taking the hippo out of her hands when she didn't move, brushing away the lone tear that trickled down her cheek. 'Though, if you cry I might have to take it back to the store.'

She chuckled, dabbing under her eyes to prevent further spillage, and delved into the box, her hands searching amongst a sea of tissue paper until she encountered a small, square box.

It felt suspiciously like jewellery, and she hesitated, suddenly nervous.

What could this mean?

Surely Nate hadn't taken his obligation to extremes and bought her a ring? He wouldn't be crazy enough to propose…?

'You're one of those infuriating go-slow people on Christmas Day, aren't you? The kind who never rip off the wrapping paper all in one go to get to the good stuff.'

She flashed him a haughty stare. 'Good things are worth waiting for.'

'Damn right,' he said, sending her another trademark sexy smile which notched up the temperature in the room by ten degrees at least.

With shaking fingers she flipped open the box, breathing a sigh of relief and wonder as she poked at the tiny gold booty nestled in white satin.

'It's gorgeous,' she said, marvelling at the intricate work, the perfection of it.

He cleared his throat, and she wondered if he felt half as choked up as she did as the enormity of what they were doing hit home.

They were going to be parents.

There would be many more opportunities like this for giving and sharing gifts with their child: birthdays, Christmases, graduations and beyond.

Special moments to be captured like a still photograph and pressed into her heart, never to be forgotten, made extra special for sharing it with a man like Nate.

'I thought you might clobber me with your laptop if

I gave you jewellery, so this way you can choose to keep the charm for the baby's bracelet if it's a girl or add it to one of your own.'

His tone, husky with emotion, had her avoiding his gaze. If she looked up and saw those dark eyes studying her, she'd burst into tears without a doubt.

'And if it's a boy?'

He chuckled. 'Okay, you got me. I really want you to have the charm. Maybe one day you'll let me buy you the bracelet to go with it?'

'Don't push your luck,' she said, sending him a mock-scathing look that withered under the intensity of his stare.

'How about a charm for every milestone of the baby's life?'

'Yeah, that sounds good. I can see it now. A dummy for the first month, a teething ring for the sixth, and a potty around two?'

Actually, she liked the idea. It was sweet and thoughtful and totally Nate.

'Though I draw the line at miniature gold forceps to commemorate the birth, okay?'

He laughed and slipped an arm around her waist. 'Come on. We have some serious schmoozing to do.'

'And later?'

His hand felt way too good resting on her hip, its warmth branding her skin through the thin chiffon, sending a powerful wake-up call to those crazy hormones which had dozed off for the last few minutes.

'I promise we'll talk,' he said, dropping an all-too-brief, too-chaste kiss on her cheek before guiding her out the door.

Resigning herself to an interminable evening of

back-slapping and fake smiles at equally fake people, she focussed on what really mattered about this evening: Nate by her side, their baby nestled safe within her belly, and the conversation with the potential to make or break her future.

'Are you having a good time?'

Kristen nodded, and tried for the umpteenth time that evening not to get lost in the dark depths of Nate's eyes.

'Actually, I am. Usually these functions are kind of dull, but with lemon-meringue pie for dessert, it's taken the evening into the next realm.'

Nate chuckled and pushed his dessert plate across to her. 'And here I was, thinking I was the reason you were having such a good time.'

'Now why would you think that?'

She batted her eyelashes at him, loving every minute of this unexpectedly enjoyable night as he laughed and pointed to the plate.

'Eat up. It's good for you,' he said, dropping his voice low as he sent a pointed stare at her belly.

'Okay. If you insist,' she said, needing little encouragement to devour a second serving of her favourite dessert.

However, she almost choked on the first mouthful as Nate's gaze stayed riveted to her lips, his expression hungry, though she had a sneaking suspicion it wasn't for food.

'Do you want some?'

His gaze stayed focussed on her lips a tad longer before slowly drifting upwards. 'No thanks. Besides, it's much more fun watching you enjoy it.'

'Uh-huh,' she said, taking her time with the next mouthful, savouring the sweet tart exploding on her tongue, her pulse racing at the hungry gleam in Nate's eyes.

Looked like her boss wanted to have his cake and eat it too!

'So, what's your favourite dessert?' She needed to say something, do something to break the sexual tension which had enveloped them in a cosy cocoon, before she did something crazy like offer him a taste of the pie…from her lips!

'Tiramisu.'

'Not bad. But not as good as this.'

'I'm starting to believe it,' he said, reaching across to dab at a meringue crumb which clung to the corner of her lips.

'Thanks,' she murmured, expecting him to deposit the crumb in his napkin, shocked when he lifted his finger to his mouth and ate it.

'You're right. Delicious,' he said, his hypnotic stare never leaving hers for an instant as his lips curved into a knowing smile.

Kristen didn't know how long they sat there, staring at each other like a couple of moonstruck teenagers, but if it hadn't been for the band starting up she knew without a doubt she would've leaned into him and kissed him.

It had been that kind of night.

A night for flirting, for chatting and for learning new things, like favourite desserts.

A night for growing closer, for fighting a losing battle with the escalating attraction sizzling between them.

A night for doing crazy things, like throwing herself at her boss.

'Would you like to dance?'

She shouldn't.

If sitting next to him was sending her body into meltdown, what hope would she have wrapped in his arms?

'I'd love to,' she said, happily ignoring her own logic and placing her hand in his.

They strolled hand in hand to the dance floor, or, more precisely, Kristen floated alongside Nate, grateful for his strong grip. The way her knees trembled, she wouldn't have made it two feet without his support.

'It's been ages since I've done this,' Nate said, taking her into his arms and cradling her close, while she struggled not to kiss the pulse point in his throat beating at her eye level.

It was so tempting…the rhythmic throb, throb, throb a beacon to her overstimulated imagination.

It would be so easy…

'Let me guess. Favourite song?'

She tore her gaze away from his throat and tried to focus on what he was saying.

'This song? You were humming it under your breath.'

Kristen had been oblivious to the music till now. In fact, they could've been dancing a polka and she wouldn't have known, wouldn't have cared, as long as she was wrapped in this incredible man's arms.

'It is a favourite. It's an Elvis classic—*Are You Lonesome Tonight.*'

His eyes widened ever so slightly. 'Is that an offer?'

She held her breath, wondering how far she could tease him, wondering if she could handle the fallout.

And there would be—she had no illusions about that. They hadn't discussed the baby yet. In fact, this evening was a mere prelude to the main event, and she shouldn't get caught up in the romance of it.

So Nate was flirting a little.

It probably didn't mean anything, and she'd be better off recognising that.

'You know it's the song title,' she said, reluctantly disengaging from his arms as the song came to an end and heading back to the table.

'My favourite's *It's Now or Never,*' he said, falling into step beside her, the laughter in his voice audible.

She rolled her eyes and smiled as he pulled her chair out and she sat down, feeling every inch a princess yet aware her Prince Charming could well turn into a frog by the end of the evening.

'I've had a good time tonight.'

Nate captured her hand, the tender expression in his eyes bringing a lump to her throat, and in total contrast to the suave, confident guy who'd been teasing her all evening.

'Me too,' she said, trying not to get too caught up in the moment, but fighting a losing battle when he interlaced his fingers with hers.

'Want to get out of this place and go have that chat?'

'You bet.'

However, as they left the Grand Ballroom with their hands intertwined, Kristen wondered if she'd have been better off living the fantasy a little longer.

After all, reality had a funny way of letting her down.

* * *

'Where are we?'

Nate turned into his street, pulled into the first house on the right and killed the engine, turning to face Kris.

'There are advantages to you not being a Melbourne girl. I can take you anywhere and it's like an adventure every time,' he said, smiling as her eyes widened with curiosity, their dazzling blue a more muted midnight in the dim car.

'Right now, this intrepid adventurer needs to use the bathroom desperately, so unless this is your house or the house of a very good friend who'll let a crazy woman bash their door in I suggest you get me to a convenience store pronto.'

He smiled, enjoying her sense of humour. It was one of the things he remembered from their brief liaison in Singapore, her dry sense of humour and the ability to laugh at herself even in the face of adversity.

'Rather than have you terrorise the good folk of Middle Park on a Sunday night, I'll let you use the bathroom. Come on.'

She almost ran all the way to the front door and he unlocked it, disarmed the alarm and pushed it open in record time, barely having time to say, 'Down the hall, last door on the left,' as she pushed past him and dashed down the hallway, her heels clattering along the boards.

Wondering what she'd think of his place and hoping she'd go for his plan he flicked on the lights, illuminating the lounge, his favourite room in the house. With its soaring ceilings, elaborate cornices and marble fireplace, the room captured the period feel of the house perfectly, and he often spent his limited own-time in here, working from his laptop in front of the fire or reading a book while stretched out on the Chippendale sofa.

Julia had loved this room too. In fact, they'd both walked into the house and known this place was perfect, making an offer to the surprised estate agent on the spot.

Battling the wave of sadness which swamped him whenever he thought of her, he picked up a picture, his favourite, depicting the two of them in the Whitsundays: smiling, joyous, without a care in the world.

Life had been pretty simple back then—work, play, live for the moment. Buying this house had been a big step towards their future, and now maybe it was time to start thinking about a future of a different kind.

'Who's that?'

Kris had slipped off her shoes and come up behind him, her eyes fastened on the picture frame.

'My wife,' he said, replacing the photo on the granite mantelpiece and quashing his old memories, knowing it was time to explain, and eager to get to the point of this evening.

However, before he could say another word, Kris paled and slumped onto the sofa, her mouth a surprised O, before her eyes clouded in confusion and flicked between the photo and his face.

'Your *wife?*'

She shook her head, bewilderment etched across her beautiful face.

CHAPTER TEN

KRISTEN struggled to process Nate's revelation, knowing there had to be a perfectly logical explanation behind this.

Nate couldn't be married. She'd worked with him for months and he spent all his time at the office. Besides, he wasn't that sort of guy, the sort that played around on his wife, having one-night stands in foreign countries, getting other women pregnant…or was he?

She knew next to nothing about him, and coming to his house accentuated the fact.

Though her knowledge of Melbourne wasn't extensive she knew Middle Park was an upper-class suburb and period homes like this cost a small fortune.

Throw in the fact that the house was the epitome of a family home, with a sprawling front lawn complete with rope and tyre hanging from an old oak tree just waiting for some child to swing from it, and the sheer size of the rooms she'd seen to date, and she knew that Nate had some explaining to do. Big-time.

'Julia died three years ago,' he said, sitting next to her on the sofa and reaching across for her hand before thinking better of it.

She scuttled away from him to the furthest corner of the sofa and folded her arms. She needed to absorb his words and touching him, indeed any kind of proximity, didn't help.

'I'm sorry,' she said softly, her trite words echoing in the cavernous room. She felt ashamed for jumping to stupid conclusions a moment ago but still annoyed she knew nothing about him.

Admittedly, it wasn't his fault. They'd agreed to forget their one night of passion, to move on to a professional footing once she'd started working at RX, but the game plan had changed thanks to the little life inside her, and the closer they'd grown at work despite all intentions otherwise.

'We were the clichéd high-school sweethearts,' he said, studying his hands clasped in his lap as if they held the answers to the world's problems. 'We dated for an eternity, taking a break once to see other people before realising we were meant to be together.'

She remained silent, biting on her inner lip to stop crying out from the pain lancing her heart. Sure, she'd wanted to know more about Nate, but this wasn't quite what she'd had in mind—listening to him offload about the love of his life.

'We got married eight years ago. That picture with Jules was taken on our honeymoon.'

Kris's folded arms tightened as she tried to give herself a comforting hug, trying to ignore the tender expression on Nate's face at his cherished memories, hating herself for being insanely jealous of a dead woman.

Right then, it hit her.

She could never compete with a ghost and, as much

as she'd tried to deny that having Nate in her life wasn't an issue, she'd been lying to herself since the moment she'd walked into his office and discovered the guy she hadn't been able to forget had re-materialised in her life.

'You must miss her very much,' she said, needing to fill the growing silence, desperate to say something before she let out an anguished groan.

He nodded, finally lifting his gaze to meet hers, and what she saw there shrivelled up any last residual hope she might have harboured of being anything more to him than his child's mother.

'I loved her like nothing else,' he said, his gaze bright with adoration. 'But she's gone, and I've had to move on.'

Kristen didn't want to dwell on how much Nate had obviously loved his wife, but she needed to know what had happened, if only to satisfy some weird curiosity to discover everything that made this enigmatic man tick.

'How did she die?'

Nate's expression hardened, his dark eyes turning glacial. 'A haemorrhage.'

'How awful,' she murmured, aware that sudden, unexpected brain haemorrhages were on the rise in young people, often with no preceding signs or symptoms.

Little wonder Nate wore an invisible cloak of sadness wrapped around his shoulders, and had since the first minute they'd met. Losing his wife so quickly, so tragically, must've really hurt and hurt deep.

Suddenly, a light bulb flashed in her head. The guilt she'd sensed after they'd slept together, the way he'd flirted with her one minute then pulled back the next, his swinging moods when they'd first started working together—it all made sense now.

He loved his wife despite the years since her death, then she'd entered the picture and thrown him for a six. Sleeping with her must've really been a big deal for him, and he'd probably tried to put it behind him only to have his night of guilty pleasure rubbed in his face when she'd walked through the doors of RX.

Trust her to fall for a guy still wrapped up in the memory of his beloved dead wife.

'It's over. It's in the past.'

He spoke softly, as if reassuring himself, and she waited, knowing that whatever she had to say next would sound inadequate.

'But that's not relevant to what I want to discuss with you tonight,' he said, louder this time, and back in control. 'Before we get into any of that, would you like something to drink?'

'No, I'm fine,' she said, wishing he'd get to the point so she could high-tail it out of here with what was left of her tattered dignity intact.

If she stayed a minute longer in this elegant room, with pretty *Jules* smiling down on her, she'd start bawling.

'I've been thinking,' he said, scooting closer to her, invading her personal space with his powerful body. 'This place is too big for one person. It's designed for a family. So what do you say to moving in? Let me take care of you during the pregnancy, and when the baby comes we can take it from there.'

She shot bolt-upright, her lower back twinging as it had been for a while now—more of those hormones, apparently, softening her spinal ligaments.

'You're kidding, right?'

He shook his head, his expression deadly serious, and she wondered if the hormones were affecting her lucidity too.

'It makes sense, Kris. Your place has all those steep stairs, and the larger you get the harder it will be to drag yourself up and down them. There's a master bedroom on the ground floor here, with a sitting room attached which would make a perfect nursery.'

'Master bedroom, huh?'

He had this all figured out.

Up until that instant she'd assumed his offer had stemmed from concern for the baby and doubts in her ability to care for it, but now he'd drawn another picture, one which involved the two of them reneging on their deal to remain platonic, and for one ridiculous second her traitorous body leaped at the idea.

'My room's upstairs, so you'll have use of the whole ground floor if you want.'

Okay, so he didn't want her body. Not that she could blame him, what with her expanding waistline, thickening ankles and the first hint of cellulite dimpling her previously toned thighs.

But that still didn't make his offer any more appealing.

It didn't make sense.

Why would a workaholic, successful guy at the top of his game want to take care of her? She wasn't exactly helpless, far from it, and though she wanted to tell him where he could shove his offer a small part of her loved him for making it.

Loved him?

Like the sun rising slowly over the horizon and

bathing the earth with an illuminating glow, the first rays of realisation filtered through her, creating warmth and amazement and havoc.

She loved him?

How could that be possible when she'd never experienced the nebulous emotion first-hand, let alone knew what it felt like?

Besides, it wasn't supposed to happen like this.

They were supposed to be two ships passing in the night, colliding for one brief interlude before moving on. However, it looked like not only had their ships docked but they'd taken on an extra passenger, one who made them both contemplate crazy things.

He wanted her to move in, and she suspected she felt more for him than the crazy crush she'd previously harboured.

Time to cast away and set sail for destinations unknown before her ship along with her dreams sunk like a stone.

'So, what do you think?'

'I think you're nuts,' she said, resisting the urge to reach out and comfort him when his face fell. 'First you ask for more time to absorb the fact you're going to be a dad. Then you give me presents which hint at your intentions to be involved but don't actually spell it out, and now you jump to this? It's crazy.'

'It's the best solution for everyone.'

She raised an eyebrow, wondering if some of her irrational hormones had taken a flying leap and landed on him.

'Thanks for the offer, but we can't live together. I've never lived with anyone, and I value my independence, as I'm sure you do. It would never work.'

His jaw tightened, a stubborn set to it. 'We'd make it work. For the sake of the baby.'

Suddenly, the pieces of the puzzle slid into place like the rumblings of tectonic plates moving into place.

'You don't think I'm capable of caring for this baby myself?'

'Don't be ridiculous,' he said, his quick look-away glance speaking volumes. 'I only want what's best for you.'

'Cut the crap, Nate. We both know you want what's best for the baby. I'm just the incubator,' she said, anger turning her words into sharp barbs intended to wound him like he'd wounded her.

'That's not fair. I care about you.'

He reached for her hand, gripping it tightly when she tried to tug away, using his other hand to tilt her chin up.

'Listen to me. I know this pregnancy is the last thing either one of us expected, but it happened and we're responsible. You wouldn't have told me about the baby if you didn't want me involved, and like it or not I'm here to stay. I'm sorry it took me a while to get my act together, but I'm one hundred percent committed now. This baby means more to me than you could possibly know, and I intend on doing everything in my power to make sure the both of you are cared for. Understood?'

The vehemence behind his impassioned words startled her. It sounded like he meant business—and a huge part of her was grateful that her baby would have a father who would love and cherish and protect it, something she'd never had after her parents had died.

'You're pretty hell-bent on this, aren't you?'

'Damn right,' he said, his fingers warm against the

tender skin under her jaw as his thumb brushed her bottom lip.

Sighing, she finally relaxed, taking hold of his hand—she couldn't take much more of that lip stroking—and squeezing both of them in hers.

'Okay, here's how it will be. I'm not moving in here, no matter what you say, but you can have full involvement in the pregnancy. Ultrasounds, obstetrician visits, antenatal classes, the works. How's that for a compromise?'

'You drive a hard bargain,' he said, his smile warming her right down to her toes. 'Sounds good. For now.'

She ignored his addendum, too tired to ram her point home. She'd never move in with Nate no matter how hard he pushed or how many logical arguments he laid out.

She wasn't a fool, and raising a child in a home where two parents didn't love each other would do much more damage than visitation rights and planned holidays.

With a weary smile, she said, 'Okay, then. Let's see some of this caring attitude starting with you taking me home. I'm beat.'

And if she didn't establish some much-needed distance between them in the next few minutes she'd be curling up on his sofa—or, worse, checking out the *upstairs* master-bedroom.

Being with Nate felt too comfortable, too cosy, too right, and hot on the heels of her startling realisation that she actually might love him it threatened to undermine her very existence.

No matter how much he cared for her, no matter how close the baby brought them, she could never compete with Julia. He'd virtually said she'd been the love of his life, and she had no intention of coming in a poor second.

She'd had enough of that feeling growing up, always playing second fiddle to a foster mum's biological kids, always the new kid on the block as she moved from school to school, always the outsider.

Never again; she'd make sure of it, even if it meant breaking her heart in the process.

'Come on, I'll take you home,' he said, gently pulling her to her feet, clasping her hands like he'd never let go.

More of that wishful thinking.

'Thanks, Nate. For everything,' she said, knowing how lucky she was to have a dependable guy as the father of her baby, a part of her wishing there could be more between them.

'You're welcome.'

He dropped a chaste kiss on her cheek, the type of kiss indicative of their relationship.

Or was it?

No matter how platonic they tried to keep their relationship, there'd been the shared moments in the office working on *Travelogue,* and as for the Logies tonight…

Nate had been at his charming best, and she'd had a hard time separating her rational side, which told her he was just being nice to her at a work do, and her emotional side, which replayed every touch, every intimate smile. And that spectacular dance where their bodies had been so very close…

She should be ecstatic they'd ironed out some major issues where the baby was concerned.

Instead, as she followed him out the door of his beautiful home and to his car, she couldn't help but wish for it all.

CHAPTER ELEVEN

'WOULD you like to know the sex of the baby?'

Nate's coal eyes clashed with Kris's, a wonder-filled smile spreading across his face.

'What do you think?'

Kris didn't know what to think.

She hadn't known what to think for a while now. Since their chat after the Logies, Nate had showered her with attention, doing considerate things like dropping by with groceries, accompanying her on walks around Albert Park Lake, even bringing her the chocolate milk-shakes she craved at all hours.

A girl could get used to this sort of treatment, and with every passing week she fell deeper for the man with a knack for lavishing some much-needed affection on her.

'I'm not sure. Would you like a surprise at the end?'

A shadow crossed his face, but before she could interpret it he said, 'Honestly? I think we've both had all the surprises we can take. I'd like to know.'

'Me too.'

She clasped his hand and turned to the doctor. 'Okay, let us have it.'

The doctor beamed as he wiped the ultrasound gel

from her belly. 'Congratulations. You have a healthy baby girl growing in there.'

'A girl,' Nate said, his voice barely a whisper as he clutched her hand.

'Wow.'

Kris let the tears flow as she sat up and thanked the doctor, who grinned at them like a generous benefactor as he handed her a photo of the baby and left the room.

'Bet she's as gorgeous as her mother,' Nate said, tracing the baby's outline with a fingertip before leaning over and placing a soft, lingering kiss on her lips.

Kris blinked, but the tears flowed heavier as he gathered her in his arms, strong and protective as the rest of him, as she tried to figure out what that tender kiss had been about.

'I take it this means you're happy?'

He drew away from her and brushed a strand of hair out of her face, his hand warm against her cheek for a brief moment.

'Very.'

She sniffled, gratefully grabbing a few tissues from the box he held out to her, wondering if she'd ever get over the urge to bawl at the slightest provocation. 'We're having a girl…'

'Pretty amazing, huh?'

Amazing? Nothing came close to the overwhelming intensity of emotions flooding her body: pride, awe and blinding love filled her till she could barely see.

Knowing the sex of the baby made it all the more real, and she could now chat to her baby girl, labelling her a 'she' rather than an unknown entity.

'This is all so unbelievable,' she said, gripping his

hand like she'd never let go, gazing down at her protruding belly with a growing sense of wonderment. 'I have a little girl in there.'

Nate reached out and rubbed his hand over her belly, like a hopeful man with an old lamp wishing for a genie.

'My girls,' he said, the sheen of unshed tears in his eyes as he looked at her, pride overpowering the momentary sadness she could've sworn she'd glimpsed earlier.

'Well, at least one of us is,' she said, pushing up to a sitting position and patting her tummy. 'Is it too early to start talking about names?'

He smiled and helped her off the bed. 'No. How about we do it over dinner?'

Kris hesitated. So far, all of the time they'd spent together had been centred on the baby, and she preferred it that way. No use fuelling her useless fantasies of Nate seeing her as anything other than the mother of his child. Having a cosy dinner for two wouldn't help her fertile imagination, especially an imagination which took his caring words 'my girls' and turned it into something more meaningful.

'I'll cook.'

He saw that as an enticement, whereas the thought of spending time holed up in his perfect house waiting for the perfect family intimidated her more than the thought of eating with him.

Darn it, she'd known falling for him would complicate matters, but she hadn't expected to feel this out of her depth all the time—lending weight to words which were meaningless, imagining more than friendship behind every touch or casual peck on the cheek, wishing he'd feel more for her.

'Sounds good,' she said, forcing a smile, when her less-than-enthusiastic tone obviously hadn't convinced him of her enthusiasm for his plan if the tiny frown between his brows was any indication. 'As long as you don't feed me Brussel sprouts and broccoli. I'm taking a vitamin supplement, and if I have one more green leafy vegetable this week I'm going to barf.'

'I thought the morning sickness had stopped ages ago?'

The teasing glint in his eyes soon had her chuckling along with him as she padded over to a screen, clutching the back of the hospital gown which threatened to give him an eyeful with every step, and slipped behind it to get dressed.

'Would you like me to bring anything?'

'Just my favourite girls.'

His voice drifted over the top of the screen, and her fingers fumbled with the last button of her blouse as she wondered if he had any idea the impact of his casual words had on her.

She couldn't see his expression, therefore couldn't ascertain whether he was serious or joking, especially as his tone gave little away.

Silently chastising herself for reading too much into his comments, she stepped out from behind the screen after sliding the last button home.

'Okay, then, let's get back to work. Alan should have the first tape of *Travelogue* ready for viewing.'

She headed for the door, brisk and businesslike, the only mode which kept her focus diverted from Nate and the mixed signals he was sending her.

'Speaking of which, are you going to announce your pregnancy today?'

She nodded, glancing down at her flowing geometric-patterned top in turquoise, black and camel. 'I'm surprised nobody's guessed yet with the loose clothes I've been wearing.'

'You look sensational as always,' he said, his admiring glance sweeping from her top to her fitted black trousers with the elasticated waist and back again. 'With a gorgeous body like yours, no one can tell you're pregnant unless they've seen your belly.'

She fidgeted under his intense stare, flattered by his words, wishing her overactive imagination wouldn't conjure up the glint of desire in his eyes.

'Well, until now you're the only one who has had that privilege, so let's spread the word before the rumour-mills start up.'

He laid a hand on her arm as she opened the door. 'You know I'm proud to be the father?'

'Uh-huh. But we've both agreed to keep the paternity a secret at work. It's nobody's business but ours, and I don't want it affecting our professional lives.'

'You sure?'

'Positive.'

It was tough enough climbing the corporate ladder, without having to fend off snide barbs from co-workers insinuating she was getting ahead because she was sleeping with the boss.

Ha!

If they only knew it had been a one-off, a distant, cherished memory she replayed at will, especially in the long, lonely hours of the morning when her bladder woke her for frequent trips to the loo and she couldn't get back to sleep for thinking about Nate.

'There is one thing you can bring to dinner tonight.'

'What's that?'

'A hat.'

She stared at his deadpan face, the corners of his mouth twitching with barely concealed amusement.

'A hat?'

'That's right. Now, let's get back to work before the boss fires your cute butt.'

Sending him a mock-angry glare, secretly thrilled about his butt comment, she followed him out of the clinic, wondering if he would ever stop surprising her.

'One hat, as requested.'

Kris placed a misshapen red beanie on the dinner table, smack bang between the silver candlestick-holders and the crystal glasses. 'Now, are you going to tell me what on earth it's for?'

Nate smiled and pulled out her chair, gesturing for her to sit.

'Well, you strike me as being a woman of firm opinions, so I thought the only way for us both to decide on a name would be to draw one out of a hat.'

She laughed, the loud, genuine sound of a woman who was happy, something he'd heard more of lately, and he hoped she'd still feel that way after he dropped his little bombshell on her tonight.

'Are you saying I'm stubborn?'

'Interpret it as you will,' he said, grinning as he filled her glass with her preferred sparkling mineral-water and lemon, increasingly grateful they could joke around like this.

They'd grown closer, had settled into a comfortable

friendship, the type of friendship he valued, the type of friendship he could easily see developing into something more given half a chance.

She sipped her mineral water and replaced it on the table, her cheeky glance alerting him to another of her trademark quick remarks. 'There won't be a problem as long as you agree with me.'

He chuckled. 'Tell me you're not into the way-out Hollywood-style names. I'm a conservative kind of guy, and I don't think I can cope with my daughter being called Apple or any other types of fruit.'

'You sound like an old man.'

'I am,' he said, feeling every one of his thirty-six years.

Gut-wrenching grief did that to a man, robbing him of optimism, joy and hope. But the remarkable woman sitting in front of him had changed all that.

Courtesy of the little miracle she was carrying, he suddenly had hope for the future. And it felt great!

'You're right. I can see quite a few grey hairs amongst all that black,' she said, pointing to the area around his temple. 'Hope you haven't passed on the premature-ageing gene to our daughter.'

'You'll keep,' he said, grinning as he pointed a finger at her before heading for the kitchen. 'Just for that, I'll serve your favourite sprouts and broccoli first.'

He half expected her to follow him into the kitchen, but as he returned with plates piled high with steaming stir-fry, and saw her sitting on the edge of her seat and fiddling with cutlery, he had to admit it would take more than a few teasing words and a home-cooked meal to get her to relax.

She'd seemed on edge the last time she'd been here,

but he'd put that down to discovering he'd been married and the strangeness of the situation. However, it looked like she hadn't loosened up at all, and if he didn't get her to unwind he had no chance of convincing her to see the wisdom of his plan.

Setting a plate down in front of her, he took a seat opposite.

'This smells fantastic,' she said, inhaling the fragrant aroma of sautéed garlic, ginger and lemon grass, the three staples he used in any stir-fry.

It was too long since he'd cooked, preferring to eat at the office or grab a quick bite on his way home.

He'd missed this, missed seeing the appreciative expression on someone's face as they took the first bite, the low 'Mmm' resonating from them as they forked more into their mouths.

Jules had loved his cooking, though with her long hours at the Playhouse he'd often ended up eating alone over the years.

However, seeing Kris's obvious enjoyment as she slurped up noodles, smacked her lips and shovelled the food into her mouth with surprising speed, more than made up for any reticence on Julia's part in the past.

A painful niggle of guilt wormed its way into his heart. He shouldn't compare the two women.

They were very different, and he'd already come to terms with the fact he needed to move on with his life.

Over the last weeks he'd wondered if Kris's unexpected pregnancy wasn't the catalyst he needed, forcing him to compartmentalise his memories and set about creating a new future.

However, to do that he'd have to tell her the whole

truth about Julia's death, and now that her pregnancy was advanced he couldn't do it.

He didn't want to scare her, and the stress of hearing the truth now couldn't be good for her or the baby. He'd have to bide his time and hope she'd understand once he told her everything.

And he would, there was no doubting that.

He'd been torn up inside for too long, guilt-ridden over possibly letting another woman into his life to usurp Julia's position. However, after long nights of soul-searching, he knew Julia wouldn't have wanted him to put his life on hold, to wallow in grief and self-pity. She'd always lived life to the full, throwing herself into their relationship with as much passion as she'd done for her roles on stage.

'Life is meant to be gobbled like a scrumptious chocolate-cake, not nibbled around the edges,' she'd used to say, and he could almost sense her now, silently egging him on to set aside the past and focus on the future.

'You haven't touched yours,' Kris said, pointing to his plate while she dabbed at her mouth, her apologetic glance flicking between her plate and him. 'Meanwhile, I've just entered the *Guinness Book of Records* for scoffing a meal in two seconds flat.'

'You know there was broccoli in that?'

Her hand flew to her mouth in mock horror. 'Really? Is that what those little green tree-shaped things were?'

He laughed, pushing his noodles around the plate before giving up and resting the fork down. No use pretending he had an appetite. Besides, he doubted he could force a mouthful of food past the giant lump stuck in his throat.

'What's wrong?'

Realising there was no time like the present, he swapped seats, sliding into the stiff-backed chair next to her. 'Nothing's wrong. But I want to talk to you about something.'

'Uh-oh. By the look in your eye, it sounds serious.'

'It is.'

He took hold of her hand, small and soft, hoping she felt one iota of what he felt for her. It was the only way he could convince her to go through with this.

'I was planning to wait till later, but I can't concentrate on anything else.'

Her eyes widened, depthless blue pools a man could drown in. 'You're starting to scare me.'

'Sorry, that's the last thing I want to do.'

Taking a deep breath, he tried not to blurt out the words he'd silently rehearsed for the entire afternoon in one go.

'I know this is going to sound crazy to you, especially after you refused my offer to move in, but I want you to consider this carefully. It's the best thing for the baby, to surround her with both parents, especially in the early formative years. She needs to feel loved and I think we can give that to her. Together.'

Gripping both her hands, staring into her incredible eyes and hoping to God he was doing the right thing for them all, he said, 'Kris, will you marry me?'

CHAPTER TWELVE

KRIS stared at Nate in horror, certain she'd heard a proposal spilling from the lips she'd spent way too much time fantasising about, her brain having a problem computing it.

'*Marry* you?'

Shaking her head, she took shallow breaths, trying not to hyperventilate at a time when she needed her wits the most.

He squeezed her hand, his voice steady when she felt like screaming. 'I know it's out of the blue, and probably the last thing you expected, but I really want us to make a go of this. To try and be a family for our daughter.'

Kris gritted her teeth so hard her jaw ached. She couldn't believe he was doing this to her—again! First the 'move in and let's play happy families' scenario and now this!

Hating the quiver in her voice, she said, 'Do you love me?'

The widening of his eyes and quick look away spoke volumes.

'I care about you, Kris. Surely you know that?'

Numb with pain, she said, 'It's not enough. I know

you care, but a marriage needs more than that. And I know you mean well, but you've just presented your proposal with all the flair of a business deal, and it's not enough. You want to take care of me and the baby? Fine. You want to lavish our daughter with love? Fine. But we don't have to be married or live together for you to do that.'

'We'd have a solid foundation for a marriage. We could build on it. We could—'

'I can't marry you, Nate. I'm sorry.'

She stood, not surprised he released her hands and moved across to the fireplace, staring into the flames while she blinked away tears before turning to face him again.

'I know you want what's best for the baby. I do too, but children pick up on emotions around them, and I don't want our daughter realising the only thing keeping her parents together is her.'

'It wouldn't be like that,' he said, his tone low and imploring as he crossed the room to stand beside her. 'Surely you feel something for me? Enough to take a chance on building a future for our daughter? To take a chance on seeing what develops?'

Pain ripped through her at the bleakness in his eyes.

Feel *something*?

She felt everything for him.

Shaking her head, she picked up her denim jacket lying on the back of the sofa and shrugged into it.

'I'm sorry, Nate. Feeling something just isn't enough. And I'm not prepared to sit around waiting for whatever we feel for each other to maybe or maybe not develop into something more. Respect, admiration, attraction, whatever we've got right now, isn't enough. I deserve more than that. We both do. I need more and I won't settle for anything less.'

Willing her legs to move towards the door, she half expected him to stop her.

Even with the empty ache spreading through her heart with every step taking her further away from him, she wanted him to stop her, to tell her this was all some huge mistake, that he did love her, and that marrying her, becoming a real family, was the most important thing in his life.

He didn't stop her, and the hollow slam of the door echoed the slamming door in her heart as she shut away her love for the man who'd broken it without trying.

'What's this?'

Nate looked up from the pile of documents on his desk and held up a letter the minute Kristen entered his office and closed the door.

Damn, she'd decided to play this cool, to be professional to the end. But seeing him sitting behind his fancy desk, with a smug expression on his face and a raised eyebrow, as if he didn't quite believe her letter was serious, spiked her temper in a second.

'Have you read it?'

'Uh-huh.'

To her annoyance, he screwed it up into a ball and lobbed it into the bin three metres away.

Forcing her hands to unclench, she marched over to his desk.

'You really should keep important documentation like resignation letters for the HR department. They'll want stuff like that for employee files.'

Folding his arms, he leaned back in his chair and fixed her with a benevolent smile.

'I'm not accepting your resignation.'

'You have no choice!'

Her voice rose and she calmed it with effort, the same effort it took not to lean over the desk and wipe that grin off his face.

'Look, I don't want to get into this with you,' she said, wishing he was more rattled, hating that he wouldn't take her seriously.

She'd thought long and hard about this since his proposal. Working with him on a daily basis with that hanging between them had made her life unbearable. She couldn't stand another second of it, let alone the remaining time left before she went on maternity leave.

'What about your maternity leave?'

Squaring her shoulders, she said, 'What about it? If I leave it doesn't matter, does it? I'll be on permanent maternity leave till I find another job.'

His eyes narrowed, and she saw his right hand flex. At last, she'd scored a reaction.

'You don't have to do this, Kris.'

'Damn right I do,' she said, finally taking a seat. It was hard to maintain a tough stance when her feet were killing her courtesy of swollen ankles.

'Is it so hard working with me?'

Her gaze snapped to his, surprised by the hint of vulnerability she glimpsed in the dark depths, and hating how her heart thawed at the sight of it.

'Honestly? Yeah, it is.'

'I thought we'd moved past the proposal?'

'You might've,' she muttered, hating the lurch of her

heart as she recalled that fateful evening, the evening where for one tiny second she'd almost believed all her dreams had come true.

However, remembering his businesslike proposal rankled, no matter how much he cared, no matter how many different ways he showed it.

Seeing him on a daily basis was exhausting emotionally, and she just couldn't do it any more.

'Let's just call it quits, okay?'

Nate pushed out of his chair and moved around the desk in a flash to squat next to her and grab hold of her hand. 'Are you just talking about the job?'

'Of course,' she said, surprised by the devastation in his eyes, the sad twist to his mouth.

'Then why? Why walk away from a job you love and are great at if you're still going to see me anyway?' Shaking his head, he grabbed her other hand till she had no option but to face him, to listen to him. 'Obviously I'm the problem here, the problem you're trying to escape, but I'm not going anywhere. I'm still going to be a part of the baby's life, so why run away? Why now?'

Because I love you.

Because it hurts too much seeing you every day, thinking about what we could have if you'd give us a real chance—not some marriage based on obligation.

Because I want us to be the family you spoke about, for real.

Hating the treacherous warmth seeping from his grip through her body, she pulled her hands out of his.

'Because it's too hard,' she finally said, her voice barely above a whisper as she stared at her folded hands lying in her lap.

'It doesn't have to be,' he said, placing a finger under her chin and gently tipping it up till she had no option but to meet his eyes.

'I don't want you to go, Kris. You mean too much to me.'

'Don't you mean the *baby?*'

He didn't deserve her bitter response, not when she could see the genuine tenderness in his eyes.

To his credit, he didn't back down, even when she pushed away his finger and broke the tenuous contact binding them.

'I'm not talking about the baby. I'm talking about you and me.'

Straightening, he stalked to the bin, pulled out her resignation letter, smoothed it out and laid it on the desk in front of her.

'I've tried to be as honest as I can with you, about everything. And I'm not letting you leave here without a fight. So, here's your letter. If it's gone by the time I come in tomorrow, I'll take it you've come to your senses. If not…' he shrugged into his jacket and picked up his briefcase '…be prepared to do battle. I'm not letting my star exec producer walk out of here no matter what she thinks.'

'You're…you…'

He silenced her indignant sputtering with a swift, fierce but all-too-brief kiss on the lips before sending her a smug grin and strolling out the door.

Nate entered the conference room carrying a huge goodie-basket filled with baby stuff, pasting a smile on his face as he fought his way through the crowd surrounding a radiant Kris.

'For the mum-to-be,' he said, placing the basket on the table, wondering how long before he could make a run for it.

Having a baby shower before Kris left had been Hallie's idea, but now that the day had arrived he couldn't be less happy if he'd tried.

He'd miss her.

A lot.

Feeling something just isn't enough.

Her words from the night he'd proposed haunted him, taunting him with their finality, implying she might feel a bit for him but that it was nowhere near enough to get her to marry him.

Until her refusal he'd had no idea how badly he wanted to provide a stable home environment for his daughter, how much he was willing to risk in perhaps opening up to the possibility of more than a platonic relationship with Kris.

Being married would've given him the opportunity to take things slow, to break down the carefully erected barriers around his heart and maybe, just maybe, take a chance on more than just caring for a woman again.

But Kris didn't see the logic in his proposal, or didn't feel enough for him to take a chance and no amount of wishing things could be different would change that fact.

She'd said she deserved more than he was willing to give—and sadly she was right—but he couldn't lie to her. He had no idea what would happen if he opened his heart to another woman, and he'd been as honest as he could.

For Kris, it wasn't enough.

'Thanks,' she said, smiling up at him, the familiar twinkle in her eyes.

Ever since he'd called her bluff over her resignation a month ago, they'd entered a weird impasse in their relationship.

He'd challenge her, she'd fire back.

She'd tease him, he'd want to kiss her senseless, till he remembered he had to keep things in the office professional.

If she'd wanted to bolt after his proposal, it didn't take an Einstein to figure out what she'd do if he hauled her into his arms as he'd wanted to do almost on a daily basis.

'Hey, boss. How about you propose the toast?'

Hallie thrust a champagne flute into his hand and he blinked, annoyed by the coy little smile playing about Kris's sensual mouth, as if she could read his thoughts.

Straightening, he addressed the room, as he'd done many times over the last few months.

'Since I've taken over here at RX I've been constantly impressed by the work ethic and camaraderie shown by all of you, as demonstrated today in this great turnout for Kristen's farewell and baby shower. As you all know, she's agreed to take a year's worth of maternity leave, and I'm hoping to lure our star executive producer back to the fold then.'

Cheers greeted his announcement, and he smiled at Kris, his heart pounding as she returned it.

'She's been a great asset to the RX team, and I know you'll all join me in wishing her and her bundle of joy all the best.'

He raised his glass in her direction, watching her throat move almost convulsively as she sipped at her apple juice, her expression stoic.

'Since you're so impressed with our work ethic, boss, does this mean you'll be shouting the bar at Manic Monday tonight?'

Several people cheered Hallie's cheeky question and he held up his hand to quieten them.

'While our impossible receptionist seems to think this station has a bottomless pit of funds, I'm willing to shout each of you a drink tonight if you get back to work within the next five minutes and actually get something done in the next two hours before knock-off time.'

As expected the conference room cleared within the prescribed time, people draining champagne and taking their cake plates with them. His staff may be the most productive, loyal lot around, but boy did they love a drink to unwind after work on a Monday.

Once Hallie, the last straggler, had given them a final cheeky smile and closed the door behind her, Nate sat next to Kris and topped up her glass with juice.

'How are you doing?'

'A little tired,' she admitted, sitting back and resting her folded arms on her belly.

Exhausted, more like it, he thought, noting the dark rings of fatigue around her eyes despite the careful use of cosmetics.

'You sure you're up for the pre-natal class tonight?'

'Positive.'

She nodded, her blonde hair falling around her shoulders, longer and softer now than when she'd first started work. 'They're going over the birth options, and I really want to be there for that.'

'Want me to pick you up?'

He threw out the offer, expecting her to refuse as

she'd done on the previous five occasions, but to his surprise she nodded.

'That would be great. I've been feeling pretty lousy today. For a while there I thought I'd have to miss my own baby shower.'

'Nothing serious?'

His calm voice belied the surge of worry within. Now that she'd mentioned it, she didn't only look exhausted she looked downright ill. Despite the sassy look she'd sent him earlier, her eyes now appeared dull, and could be indicative of something more serious such as a virus. Her pallor wasn't disguised by blush.

She rubbed her belly and grimaced. 'No, I'm okay. Just the odd Braxton-Hicks contraction.'

Suddenly, it hit him.

She was scared, probably petrified, by the fake contractions that sometimes preluded the real thing.

He reached for her hand instinctively, desperate to reassure her. 'It's going to be okay. Trust me.'

Her gaze settled on their hands, her body inert, before she finally turned her hand over in his and hung on for dear life.

'I do.'

Two little words, whispered into the fraught silence, encapsulating every hope and dream he'd had for the two of them.

He'd wanted to hear her utter those words in a different context, but for now this would have to do.

He needed to be there for her, to shunt aside his own fears as her due date grew near, and concentrate on being strong for the both of them.

'You stay here and I'll load this stuff into your car then drive you home, okay?'

She nodded and slowly withdrew her hand from his. 'Nate?'

Resting a basket filled to the brim with soft toys on his hip, he said, 'Yeah?'

'I couldn't have done this without you.'

He smiled, sensing the vulnerability underlying her words, knowing he needed to reassure her now more than ever.

'Yeah, you could. You're superwoman. You just hide away your cape and wear that dodgy underwear on the inside.'

He headed for the door, thankful he'd made her smile, hoping it stayed there for the weeks ahead leading up to the birth.

Kristen tried to concentrate as the nurse facilitator droned on and on about epidurals, forceps, episiotomies and a host of other not-so-fun things she might have to look forward to at the birth of her baby.

Women in the group winced and crossed their legs for most of the talk, which she found incredibly funny, considering it was way too late for that.

As for the men, most had paled when the nurse had passed around the forceps, and some had left the room when the actual birth video had been screened.

Nate had stayed by her side through it all, his expression focussed and resolute, as if he didn't want to miss a second. She could've admired him for it if it weren't for the constant nagging ache in the middle of her back and the fact she blamed him for putting it there.

Irrational? Maybe, considering she'd been more than a willing participant in their unforgettable night in Singapore. But as the birth grew closer and her fears escalated accordingly it only seemed fitting to blame every little thing on the guy who had put her into this predicament.

'How're you holding up?' he murmured as the nurse passed around lifelike dolls to the couples, along with a bundle of cloth nappies each.

'So far so good,' she said, handing him the doll with all the finesse of a rugby player making a pass. 'Though I think it's your turn for nappy duty tonight.'

'No worries.'

Sending her a confident grin, he whipped off the doll's threadbare clothes and folded a nappy as they'd been taught at the last class. However, his skilful demonstration came undone as he attempted to fasten the nappy, involving some slick manoeuvring of the doll's leg which resulted in the leg detaching from the body.

'Oops. I better keep a close eye on you when it's time for you to look after the real thing.'

She'd meant it as a joke, but Nate didn't laugh. In fact, he didn't move or do much of anything apart from stare in horror at his hand holding the leg.

'Hey, it's no big deal. These dolls are worn out. You'll be great with our daughter.'

They had briefly discussed some names, but still hadn't got round to naming the baby yet, and she knew they'd have to tackle that potentially touchy subject in the coming weeks. Though she hadn't told him yet, she did favour slightly alternative names in favour of the stodgy old-faithfuls, and it looked like another battle loomed on the horizon.

'I need to get out of here,' he said, thrusting the doll's leg at her, his dark eyes stark and haunted. 'I'll meet you outside in half an hour.'

'Nate, it's okay—'

She didn't get to finish her sentence, as he fled the room like a man with a million demons on his tail, leaving her holding a one-legged doll and trying to ignore the ten pairs of curious eyes focussed on her.

So he'd run out on her.

It wasn't like it hadn't happened to her before. Though Nate had never abandoned her or let her down, unless she counted the crucial fact he didn't love her.

They'd pretended his proposal had never happened, but as the baby had grown and it had been increasingly difficult to sleep, she'd often thought back to that night and played the 'what if' game.

What if he'd felt more for her?

What if the proposal had been fuelled by love and passion rather than caring and obligation?

What if she was the type of woman to not give a damn anyway, and take what he offered?

Many couples had marriages based on a lot less than the mutual respect and caring she and Nate shared, but she couldn't do it. She couldn't tie herself to a man who didn't love her, no matter how solid and dependable he was.

Besides, she'd promised to be the best mother she could, and that meant being happy and content—two emotions she'd have to fake if forced to live in a sham marriage with the man she loved.

'Is everything all right, dear?'

Kristen nodded at the kindly nurse who had concern in her eyes. 'Yes. I'm fine.'

The nurse looked doubtful as she moved on to the next couple, casting the occasional glance over her shoulder as if Kristen might follow suit and bolt—okay, waddle—out the door after Nate.

Sorely tempted, she settled back in her seat, constantly wriggling as the pain in her back fluctuated from bearable to agonising, not hearing a word the nurse said as her thoughts centred on Nate and the way he'd reacted to the doll breaking.

That was no ordinary reaction.

He'd practically freaked out, so much so that he wouldn't have been able to stay for the rest of the class. She might've expected that reaction at the actual birth, but losing it over a doll's leg?

There was something drastically wrong and, though she couldn't fathom his reasons for bolting like a dad who'd just discovered he had quadruplets rather than twins, come the end of the class she'd find out.

CHAPTER THIRTEEN

'DO YOU mind telling me what your vanishing act was all about?'

Kristen barged right up to Nate in the hospital foyer, just stopping short of stabbing his chest with her finger. 'Because, the way I see it, there's no way you'd get that upset and miss the rest of the class over breaking a doll—so what's the deal?'

'Let's talk somewhere more comfortable.'

He took hold of her arm and, rather than pulling away as was her first instinct, she let him lead her to his car. No use letting pride get in the way of a little support, especially considering her back chose that moment to remind her it didn't fancy her carrying around the extra fourteen kilos or so.

'Don't you dare think about starting that engine till you've explained everything,' she said, turning to face him once they'd settled in the car.

'We can talk at your place,' he said, running a hand over his eyes as if to block her out.

Fat chance.

'No way. Start talking. Now.'

'It's complicated.'

He fiddled with his keys, jiggling them in his hand till she reached out and grabbed them.

'You've tried that one on me before, and I've got to admit it's sounding about as tired as I feel.'

Sighing, he closed his eyes for a moment and rested his head against the headrest.

'When I told you Julia died, I didn't tell you everything.'

Kristen's heart stilled at the audible pain in Nate's voice.

'She was pregnant at the time.'

'Oh, Nate.'

Kristen reached out blindly, wanting to touch him, to comfort him, to do whatever she could to take away half the agony he must be going through.

Opening his eyes, he turned to face her, his expression unreadable in the darkness of the car.

'I know I overreacted back there. Stupid, isn't it? How such a small, insignificant thing like that can ram home how inadequate I felt over Julia's death and the fact I couldn't save her or our child.'

Grasping his hand tightly, her heart aching for him, she injected as much warmth, as much love, as she dared into her voice.

'You can't blame yourself for what happened. I can't begin to understand the heartache you must've gone through over losing your wife and your child, but medical stuff happens. Stuff you can't explain or change or fix, no matter how much you want to. And, for what it's worth, I'm here for you, and I know you're going to be a great dad for our daughter.'

'Thanks.'

She caught a glimmer of his smile in the wan light and squeezed his hand, wondering what else he had to say when he opened his mouth before quickly shutting it again.

'Is there something else?'

'I'm worried about the birth,' he said, his voice unsteady as he raised worried eyes to hers. 'I hate feeling out of control when I can organise the rest of my life with ease. It's tough.'

Her heart turned over at his honest response. She understood exactly what he was feeling. For a girl who bordered on being a control-freak herself, she wasn't so rapt about the whole 'unexpected scenarios' thing the nurse had stressed in the birthing class.

'So you're admitting you're scared?'

She thought he'd lie, do the macho thing and fob her off with some lame platitude. Instead, he surprised her by taking hold of her other hand, his grip tight.

'Terrified,' he said, his expression matching the feeling perfectly.

'What happened to you being the solid one for us both? What about all those "she'll be right" pep talks you've given me?'

He shrugged, a hint of a smile playing about his mouth.

'As I remember, you told me to be quiet the last time I tried to give you a confidence boost, though in much more blunt terms.'

She smiled, releasing his hands before she did something stupid like haul him over the console and hug him to death. 'Must've been the hormones talking.'

'We're going to get through this. You know that, right?'

She rolled her eyes, determined to lighten the mood.

She had enough to worry about, without Nate freaking out and turning into a reedy sap rather than the strong oak she'd grown to depend on.

'Of course we will. As long as you don't buy our little girl any dolls for Christmas, we'll be fine.'

He finally smiled, a rueful expression erasing the lines fanning from the corner of his eyes like a worry map.

'You're not going to let me forget that episode ever, are you?'

'Nope.'

'If you bring it up at her twenty-first, I may have to ensure you never work in the TV industry again.'

She waved away his remark with a smirk. 'I'll be a millionaire by then, living off my name alone, consulting for the best producers in town.'

'Yeah?'

'Yeah,' she said, realising they hadn't traded banter like this in way too long.

They'd been too busy treading on eggshells around each other, all their conversations focussed on the baby and little else.

This felt good. Way too good, and the baby kicked at that precise moment as if reminding her it couldn't last.

'I like a confident woman,' he said, holding out his palm for the keys.

'And I like a man who admits to a doll phobia,' she said, plopping the keys into his hand and chuckling when he snatched them away, inserted them in the ignition and started the car with a roar.

'I'm never going to live this down, am I?'

'You said it,' she said, settling back into the plush leather seat, content to concentrate on the inner glow fuelled by the thought of them being together at their daughter's twenty-first.

A lot could happen in that time—including convincing the gorgeous man beside her what he was missing out on by not giving them a chance.

A real chance, based on love and sizzle, rather than an obligatory proposal reeking of old-fashioned chivalry.

Time would tell, and right now it was enough to hope and dream and look to a future filled with a bouncing baby girl and Nate by her side.

Nate knocked on Kris's door for the second time, pounding the brass knocker longer and louder before peering through the sheer curtains lining the front window.

A strange sense of foreboding crept through him as he scanned the empty room, wondering why she wasn't answering the door.

She'd been expecting him, had chewed him out for five minutes about installing the car seat in her car before her due date next week, and he'd hurried over, the slightly hysterical edge to her voice filling him with concern.

When he rapped on the window and got no response, he vaulted the side fence and ran to the back door, relieved to find the flimsy catch unlatched.

'Kris? You in here?'

He entered the kitchen, trying to keep a lid on his sky-rocketing blood pressure. There could be a perfectly logical explanation why she hadn't answered the door: she could be taking a bath to ease her back pain, or making another of her frequent toilet stops.

However, as he entered the hallway and spied her

inert form slumped over the bottom stair, sheer unadulterated panic shot through his system and he ran towards her, haunted by a terrifying sense of *déjà vu*.

'Please, God, no,' he muttered, reaching for her, feeling for a pulse in her neck, almost sagging with relief when he found one.

Gently turning her into the recovery position, he fumbled for his mobile and dialled an ambulance, praying harder than he ever had in his life.

Brushing back her hair, he bent over her, whispering in her ear. 'Kris, I know you can hear me. Everything's going to be fine. We have a precious baby girl waiting for her mum to wake up and give me another verbal spray about something, so come on. Wake up, you hear me?'

Her eyelids flickered, and for a second hope overrode the adrenalin surging through his body. But she didn't open her eyes. She didn't do anything apart from lie there, looking too still, too lifeless.

He knew he should check for blood, but he couldn't do it. Seeing her like this was tearing him apart; he couldn't face the possible evidence that she was losing their baby too.

Sirens grew closer, and he dropped a kiss on her lips before rushing to the door and opening it for the paramedics.

'She's in there.'

He pointed to the woman he loved, frozen like a statue as they went to work on her, their precise movements calming yet terrifying at the same time.

Right then, it hit him as he watched the paramedics fiddle with pressure cuffs and stethoscopes and a whole host of intimidating medical paraphernalia skimming over Kris's body.

He loved her.

Wholeheartedly. Unreservedly. Terrifyingly.

And, as much as he loved their unborn daughter, even if the unthinkable happened and she didn't survive he would still love Kris and everything she'd become to him.

'How many weeks is she?'

'Thirty-nine,' he said, knowing the baby could be delivered safely now.

If the baby was still alive.

At that moment, Kris's eyelids fluttered open, her bright blue eyes fixing on him.

'What's going on?' she said, struggling to sit up, confusion clouding her beautiful features.

'I'm guessing you fainted,' the older paramedic said, casting Nate a look between exasperation and congratulation.

'Not again,' she said, rolling her eyes and sending a horrified look at her dress hiked up around her waist. 'Is the baby all right? Did I do any damage in the fall?'

The female paramedic laid a reassuring hand on her arm. 'The baby is fine. The heartbeat is steady and strong.'

'Thank God.'

Kris's whisper slammed into him, reinforcing his own overwhelming relief. He crossed the short distance separating them, crouching down to her level, torn between wanting to bundle her into his arms and hug her breathless, and shaking her silly for scaring him like that.

'Do you have gestational diabetes?'

The female paramedic squatted down next to him and

took Kris's blood pressure, while the other paramedic repacked the emergency case.

Kris shook her head, and he forced himself not to reach out and smooth the tousled blonde waves back from her face.

'No, though my blood sugar has dipped a few times. The doc told me to pop a jelly bean or barley sugar every time I felt woozy. I was just heading to the kitchen when I must've passed out.'

'Well, your blood pressure's fine, as are the rest of your vitals.' The paramedic slid the pressure-cuff off her arm and tucked it away in her jacket of a hundred pockets. 'You should be fine, but take it easy, okay? This bub wants its mum in tip-top shape when he or she makes its grand entrance into the world.'

'She,' Nate and Kris said in unison, their eyes meeting, hers luminous, his relieved.

He'd never known relief till she'd opened her eyes a few minutes ago, the relief backed up by the paramedics pronouncing the baby was fine.

Whatever the cause of her collapse, he knew one thing for sure—he wasn't going to let her out of his sight ever again.

She could kick, she could scream, she could threaten to tell every media outlet in Australia about the infamous doll incident, but he wasn't taking no for an answer this time.

They belonged together, now and for ever.

'Right, we'll leave you folks to it,' the male paramedic said, flanking Kris's other side as they helped her to her feet and to the nearest chair. 'Take care.'

'Thanks,' she said, colour returning to her cheeks as

he sent her a glare which read 'sit there and don't move a muscle', before escorting the paramedics out the door and returning to the lounge.

'You look mad.'

She pointed to the chair next to her, and he marvelled at her resilience while smiling at her bossiness.

Nothing kept this woman down: a move from one country to another, discovering the man she'd probably wanted to forget was her new boss, an unexpected pregnancy, and the odd collapse here or there thrown in for good measure.

She was remarkable. Little wonder he'd fallen for her, even if it was the last thing he'd wanted to do.

'I'm not mad,' he said, taking a seat next to her, wondering if he should go for the direct approach—which he'd tried and failed before—or lead into it gently.

She leaned across and placed a hand on his forearm, her palm cool against the heat of his skin.

'Look, I know I must've given you a scare when you came in and found me like that. But I'm fine. The baby's fine. No use getting that look.'

'What look?'

The corners of her mouth twitched, and he could hardly restrain himself from closing the short distance between them and covering her lips with his. 'The same look you got before you asked me to move in with you, the same look before your proposal.'

Her other hand reached up and she traced a slow, sensuous path between his brows. 'You get this funny little frown-line right here. It alerts me to the fact you're about to say something profound.'

'I am.'

He missed her touch as she sat back and folded her arms, resting them on her swollen belly.

'Okay, let me have it. What is it this time—you think I should have a water birth? You've hired a police escort to take us to the hospital when the time comes? You—'

'You talk too much,' he said, leaning across the chair-arm and kissing her, angling his head for better access, his libido firing on all cylinders as she melted under him, opening her mouth to him.

He could've kissed her like this for ever, her lips warm and pliant, her hands clutching his shirt like she'd never let go. If he had his way, she wouldn't.

The fire they'd created in Singapore had been nothing like this mind-blowing, raging inferno which spread like wildfire and threatened to consume them both.

He'd tried denying the sizzling attraction back then, and his good intentions had ended up like his discarded underwear on the floor of his hotel room.

He'd never believed in fate. Yet some indefinable force had led him to this woman, to this shattering moment when his heart unfurled and swelled with love, a feeling he'd shunned for too long.

Whatever had brought this amazing woman into his life, he couldn't believe his luck, and he'd make sure she knew it every day.

'Whoa!' Her fingers relaxed from their death-grip and her palms splayed across his chest as she pulled back slightly, her lips rosily plumped and her sparkling eyes wide with shock. 'What was that all about?'

'Would you believe I thought you needed mouth-to-mouth?'

She smiled. 'Try again, wise guy.'

'Would you believe I've just eaten a jelly bean and thought you could use the sugar boost?'

She arched an eyebrow. 'Come on, you can do better than that.'

'Would you believe I love you, I want to marry you and I want us to be a real family—you, me and our daughter?'

Her face fell, her eyes hardening to icy blue as she dropped her hands into her lap.

'That's not funny.'

'It's not a joke,' he said, desperate to make her see how genuine he was, how much she meant to him. 'I want us to be together.'

He'd known she'd be a hard sell, but her frigid expression could have frozen him solid if he'd been wet.

'You'd do anything to protect this baby, wouldn't you?'

'No…yes… Hell.'

He rubbed a hand over his face, wishing this were a bad dream and he'd wake up to find Kris nestled in his bed, smiling up at him with love and affection.

'Yes, I'd do anything to protect our baby, but this isn't about that. This is about us. This is about me first falling under your spell in Singapore. This is about me being unable to sleep at night for thinking about you, for missing you, for wanting more for us but being too scared to grab it, too scared to face up to my feelings.'

Her glacial expression thawed to semi-cold. 'I don't get it. Why didn't you tell me any of this before? Why did you let me walk away after I knocked back your last proposal?'

He sighed, having known it would come to this.

Having known he'd have to tell her the whole truth if he wanted to win her love.

'You know that suitcase you had when I first met

you? Well, I carry around enough baggage which would make that look like a thimble.'

Sadness flickered in her eyes. 'This has to do with Julia, doesn't it?'

He nodded, regret filling him that he hadn't told Kris everything. It would've saved him a lot of trouble and a lot of heartache. He'd loved Julia with all his heart, but what he felt for Kris went way beyond that.

In a way the depth of his feelings for her had scared him beyond belief, but now that he'd come to his senses he couldn't stand for them to be apart a second longer.

Before he could speak, she placed a finger on his lips and shushed him.

'You don't have to say it. I know she was the love of your life. I know you'll never get over her. You say you love me, but can you look me in the eye and say it's the same love you had for her?'

'No, it's—'

'Aaahh!'

Her groan filled the air, chilling his blood as she doubled over and gripped under her belly, all colour draining from her face.

'The baby?'

She nodded, her lips turning blue from being compressed so hard, before another guttural groan tore from her throat.

'Damn it, I wish those paramedics had stuck around,' he muttered, kneeling in front of her and capturing her face in his hands. 'Kris, look at me. Is your hospital bag upstairs in your bedroom?'

'Yesss,' she gritted out, pain contorting her features while he attempted to smooth away the lines.

'Okay, I'll grab it and then we'll head to the hospital. I need you to breathe through the contractions and try to relax.'

'Just get the bloody bag,' she said, every ounce of her pain concentrated into the killer look she sent him.

He ran up the stairs, knowing her language might get a lot more expressive before the birth was over.

The birth… He was going to be a dad…hell!

Sprinting into her room, he grabbed the small wheelie-suitcase near the door and headed down the stairs, taking two at a time.

Not surprisingly, she hadn't moved, gripping onto the arms of the chair so hard her knuckles stood out.

'How far apart are they?'

'I don't know! I'm not wearing my watch,' she said, her petrified gaze locking with his, and he dropped a quick kiss on her head before bolting to his car, shoving her case in the back and running back to the house.

It was the damnedest thing, almost as if he were having an out-of-body experience, watching this crazy man running all over the place, yet totally focussed on the woman waddling down the path, leaning heavily on his arm and doubling over as they reached the car.

'Come on, sweetheart. We'll be at the hospital in five minutes,' he said, handing her into the car as another contraction hit and she almost broke his wrist with her grip.

'Make it two,' she said, resting her head back and closing her eyes, one hand rubbing the top of her belly while the other circled beneath.

Nate considered himself a careful driver, but when Kris let out the loudest groan yet he floored it, cutting lanes, copping two-finger salutes and tooting horns left, right and centre as he screeched into the hospital and pulled up in front of Emergency.

'Hurry!' she moaned, her head thrashing side to side and he made a dash for the entrance, grabbing the first nurse he could find and pointing to his car. 'The baby's coming! Now! Do something!'

To the nurse's credit, she made efficient hand-signals at the receptionist, who summoned an orderly with a wheelchair and a doctor within two seconds.

'Calm down, sir. Everything's going to be all right.'

Was it?

He had no idea.

Everything was happening so fast, and he hadn't even had a chance to tell Kris how much she meant to him. What if something happened to her? What if she went through this daunting experience thinking he loved her less than Julia?

'Naaate!'

Kris's ear-piercing scream had him sprinting after the wheelchair and into a small room off the emergency room.

The next five minutes happened in a blur as a grim-looking doctor bustled in, checked Kris's dilation and pronounced her two-centimetres dilated.

Only two? *Two?*

A little piece of Nate curled up and died deep inside as he held her hand, watching her grunt and sweat and moan her way through the next contraction, knowing there would be many more before their daughter was born, as the stuff he'd absorbed in pre-natal class came back.

The cervix needs to be dilated ten centimetres before the next phase begins.

He distinctly remembered the midwife conducting the classes teaching them that, the figure particularly sticking in his head because ten centimetres had sounded awfully big to him.

Kris whimpered and he squeezed her hand, wishing he could do more, wishing he could take away her pain, wishing he could do something other than sit here like a big, useless dummy.

As if reading his mind, she fixed him with an angry stare. 'You being here is enough, so don't go getting any ideas to bolt on me, you hear?'

He smiled, trying not to wince as pain contorted her beautiful features. 'I'm not going anywhere, even if you call me every name under the sun.'

She gritted her teeth and gripped his hand tight as another contraction rippled through her belly, her pallor and perspiration-covered face combining to leave him feeling like he'd been kicked in the gut.

'You better remember that,' she bit out, relaxing back onto the pillows and easing her death grip on his hand as the contraction passed. 'If this is only the beginning, I feel a lot of swearing coming on—most of it directed at you for getting me into this predicament in the first place.'

There was no malice behind her words. If anything, the cheeky glint in her eyes surprised him.

'As I recall, we were both pretty involved at the time.'

Their gazes locked and held as memories of their night in Singapore washed over them, notching up the temperature in the birthing suite in an instant.

'We never got to finish our talk,' she said, a small, serene smile playing about her lips, begging him to reach forward and cover them with his own.

However another ripping contraction vanquished that urge in an instant, and their shared moment of intimacy was lost.

Nate had never been a clock watcher, putting in the required hours at work without giving it a second thought. But over the next eight hours he couldn't tear his gaze away from the large, ugly kitchen-clock stuck on the wall in front of him as he rubbed Kris's back, offered her ice chips to suck and bore the brunt of her increasingly fraying temper.

'Nate, I don't think I can do this any more…'

Her whispered plea for reassurance slammed into him, and his gut turned over as he leaned forward and stroked her forehead, needing the physical contact for reassurance as much as she did.

'You're doing great, sweetheart. You're amazing. Hang in there. Our daughter is on her way.'

He hated how inadequate he sounded, how totally pathetic, and he turned in desperation to the midwife as she entered the room, silently imploring her to give them good news.

The midwife, way too calm and cheery, bustled about with ferocious efficiency, pronounced Kris ten-centimetres dilated and instructed her to push.

'There is a slight problem, dear.'

Nate's heart stopped as he stared in open-mouthed horror at the midwife, who so casually delivered news that could be catastrophic. As he'd already learned, there were no 'slight' problems with birthing; they tended to be major ones, and he hoped to God this wasn't anything serious.

'Though the baby is head down, her head is facing

the wrong way. In these cases, usually with a bit of pushing, the little mite will automatically turn and come out quickly. So we'll give it a go, shall we?'

'What's with the "we" business?' Kris muttered, sending the midwife one of the dangerous looks she'd been reserving for Nate up till that point.

In the midst of his anxiety she managed to ellicit a smile out of him, albeit a weak one, and he copped an angry glare for his trouble too.

'You're almost there, sweetheart.'

He leaned over and kissed her on the cheek, half expecting her to push him away or whack him for his trouble. Instead, she surprised him by cupping his cheek for an all-too-brief instant before the next contraction took her breath away and the roller-coaster of pain began again.

And again… And again…

Minutes stretched into hours, hours into an interminable stretch of moans and groans as he helplessly watched the woman he loved go through unbearable agony.

He barely remembered the midwife hooking up a foetal monitor over Kris's belly; he barely remembered passing Kris the nitrous oxide to help with the crest of the increasingly painful contractions. But when the baby's heartbeat started to slow with every push he rocked out of the chair and marched across to the worried midwife, who was in deep conversation with the obstetrician who'd just entered the room.

'You've got to do something now!' he said, casting frantic glances back at Kris lying in a sweaty, pale heap on the bed, hating his helpless frustration more than anything.

'We're taking her to Theatre shortly,' the obstetrician said, giving him a comforting pat on the arm which came across decidedly condescending. 'An anaesthetist is on their way up.'

'What's going on?'

Kris's shout made them both jump, and he followed the obstetrician back to the bed, his eyes glued to the foetal monitor, petrified when the heartbeat slowed yet again.

'We're taking you to Theatre shortly. We don't let our mums go longer than twenty-four hours, and you've done a mighty job, Kris. However, this little girl of yours isn't turning, so I'll try forceps, and if that doesn't work we'll be doing a Caesarean, okay?'

Nate expected Kris to protest, remembering how pro-natural she'd been about the birth throughout the ante-natal classes, but she merely nodded and slumped back, exhaustion rendering her speechless.

'Let's do it, Doc,' he said, grateful for some positive action, not quite believing Kris had been in labour for almost a day.

The rest happened in a blur: the trip down to Theatre, gowning-up himself, the obstetrician smiling when the forceps worked, and asking Kris to give one last, al-mighty push.

Suddenly, his breath caught as the doctor held up a red-faced, screaming little girl covered in white gunk, and he would've forgotten how to breathe if Kris hadn't burst into noisy tears at that moment.

'She's beautiful, just like her mother,' he whispered, tears filling his eyes as he pushed away the damp strands of hair stuck to Kris's face and kissed her on the mouth.

'Oh, Nate.'

Her sobs subsided but the tears continued, flowing down her cheeks and plopping softly on the bed, as their bundled daughter was placed in her arms and he found his own tears falling softly on the baby's blanket. 'She's incredible.'

Leaning forward, he cuddled them close, filled with an indescribable love for his girls.

'We never did get around to choosing a name,' Kris said, nuzzling the top of the baby's head with her nose, while he traced the soft curve of his daughter's cheek.

'Later,' he said, wanting to capture this moment in time for ever. 'I love you both so much.'

Thankfully, Kris didn't argue as they formed a protective circle around the baby with their linked hands.

CHAPTER FOURTEEN

KRIS pretended to sleep as Nate crept into her room and over to the cot, his voice barely a whisper as he greeted his daughter.

'Hey, little one. Hope you're being good for Mummy. She needs her rest, and so do you.'

He had that right.

She hadn't had a moment's peace since the birth, what with midwives teaching her to breastfeed, trying to express a nonexistent milk supply and learning how to bathe her gorgeous girl.

Then there was Nate—always hanging around, doting over her and the baby, reminding her of how amazing he was and of what she couldn't have.

'You know, I bet your half-brother is looking down on you right now. He's your guardian angel.'

She stiffened, wondering if the analgesia they'd given her for the episiotomy stitches had affected her comprehension.

'I never got to hold him like I have you. Guess I was too scared, but I've regretted it every day since. Babies need to be held, and I promise to cuddle you every single day.'

Kris opened her eyes, unable to lie there and pretend she hadn't heard the gut-wrenching pain in Nate's voice.

'You had a son?'

Nate jumped and swivelled to face her, his face cloaked in shadows.

'I never got to that part, did I?'

He sat on the edge of the bed and took hold of her hand, glancing across at the cot with love radiating from his eyes.

'Tell me now,' she said, happy to have her hand held, enthralled by the emotional bond created from having had the man she loved stand by her every second of the labour ordeal.

Meeting her eyes directly, he said, 'You know Julia was pregnant when she died. I wanted to tell you the rest, but I didn't want to scare you, what with the way she died. I'd been away with work and came home to find her bleeding on the kitchen floor. She'd had a placental abruption, where the baby dies and she haemorrhaged quickly. They were both dead.'

'Oh, my God. I'd assumed it was a brain haemorrhage.'

Now she understood the stricken look on his face when he'd hovered over her after she'd passed out on the stairs. He'd probably thought he was walking in on the same tragic scenario all over again.

He shook his head. 'I blamed myself. If I'd been there for her, hadn't gone to work that day, maybe I could've done something, prevented their senseless deaths in some way—but I wasn't, and I'll never forgive myself for that.'

He looked away, his glassy stare fixed on some point

over her left shoulder, and she remained silent, unsure
what to say, knowing whatever words she mumbled out
loud would sound trite and inadequate.

'I've lived with the guilt for a long time, shutting
myself off from everything but work, focussing all my
energy on business, numbing the pain of feeling. Then
you came along.'

She shook her head, dread creeping through her exhausted body. He'd said he'd loved her before the birth,
and now she finally understood.

Nate had shut down emotionally since losing Julia
and their child. Kris had given him what he wanted
most, another child, and he'd confused his awakening
emotions with love.

He didn't love her—he couldn't.

How could he love her when he was still grieving?
He'd just said he could never forgive himself; how did
he expect to move on?

'You don't have to explain anything to me, Nate. I
get it.'

'No, you don't. Sure, I've been battling the daily
guilt of not being there for Julia, but I've been fighting
an added guilt too. The guilt of moving on, of letting
Julia go, of possibly loving another woman, of acknowl-
edging that I love you more than I loved her.'

Kris's jaw dropped, and she didn't resist when he
reached up and tipped a finger under her chin to close it.

'I already told you, Jules and I were high-school
sweethearts. It's only now I realise that our love was
based on friendship, rather than the inexplicable connection you and I've had since we first met. What I feel for
you is richer, deeper, more profound than anything I felt

for Julia, and I've been beating myself up over it till I realised something. It's okay to love you, to feel good again, to start living my life, rather than using my guilt as an excuse to push you away.'

Hope unfurled in her heart, uncertain and fluttering and making her head feel lighter than any pain relief could have.

'I love you, Kris. You're everything to me.'

His kiss slanted across her lips, a gentle kiss of persuasion, and she responded as if someone had lit a rocket under her, sliding her hands around his neck and pulling him up the bed, desperate to get closer, throwing all her pent-up emotions into the kiss she'd been awaiting for ever, the incredibly special, once-in-a-lifetime kiss of a man who truly loved her.

'You know I love you too?'

She traced his bottom lip with her fingertip, enjoying his blatant shock.

'Actually, I thought we had a few sparks, and I hoped you'd grow to love me.'

'Too late. It's already happened,' she said, snapping her fingers and injecting all the love she had in her heart for him into a dazzling smile. 'Seems like I've loved you for ever.'

'For ever, huh?'

Capturing her face in his hands, he brushed a tantalising kiss across her lips. 'Sounds good to me. That's how long we've got to love each other, to create the happy family we deserve.'

He'd said the magic words—love and happy family—and Kristen melted into his embrace, knowing there could be no better place than in his protective arms. The safeness he made her feel finally banished the shadows left on her soul by her childhood, a childhood she had yet to tell him about, but the lack of love in her past seemed less important now than the love being offered to her here and now. And there would be time, time to fill each other in on the past, in a future that they would now share.

'You're going to marry me, right?'

Kristen pretended to think about it as Nate kissed his way very, very slowly up her neck, stopping to lavish some extra attention on the sensitive spot there.

'You can't keep me dangling for ever, you know. I don't want to be proposing at Maeve's twenty-first.'

'You know I love that name, right?' She smiled; choosing the name had been easy once they had met their daughter. 'And it's so perfect to have our little girl named after your mum, especially as she'll never get to meet her granddaughter.'

A shadow flickered across Nate's dark eyes. 'Mum would've loved her as much as we do. Now, stop trying to distract me by getting all sentimental and tell me your answer.'

'I thought I'd already answered you.'

She leaned down and rubbed noses with him Eskimo-kiss style, loving their closeness, the teasing, the one hundred percent security being with a guy like him brought.

For a girl who'd craved stability her whole life she'd finally found it, all wrapped up in one incredible package.

He tightened his arms around her waist, squeezing the breath out of her till she could hardly breathe.

Or was that sexy glint in his dark-as-coal eyes telling her she was pushing her luck?

'You haven't given me an answer. What with you threatening to walk out on me after my first proposal, then scaring the life out of me by collapsing, closely followed by Maeve's birth just as I'm professing my undying love to you, we haven't got around to discussing the important stuff—like weddings.'

She arched a brow, sending him the sassy look he loved so well.

'So you're pretty confident there's going to be a wedding, huh?'

'You bet.'

His fingers skimmed her spine, his feather-light touch scattering goose bumps all over, and she shivered, preening under his touch, wishing this could go on for ever.

'In that case, who am I to stand in the way of your pushy nature?'

They grinned at each other like a couple head over heels in love, knowing there'd never been any doubt about them getting married once they'd declared their love, enjoying playing the game.

'Is it kosher to marry the boss?'

'You're not my boss any more,' she said, slanting a long, slow kiss across his lips, the type of kiss guaranteed to light a fire between them. 'I'm on maternity leave as of now, remember?'

His hands framed her face as the kiss ended, his dark eyes glowing with passion in the surreal dawn light. 'I love you so much.'

'Right back at you.'

Her eyes filled with tears, and he wiped them away with a gentle fingertip. 'Still those damn hormones, huh?'

'Yeah. They make me do crazy things.'

'As long as you don't fall out of love with me when they wear off, I'll be happy.'

'Not a chance, my love. Not a chance.'

'So do you want to wait till Maeve's walking so she can be flower girl at our wedding?'

'Hell, no! I need to make an honest man out of you asap.'

'How soon?'

He traced her cheek, toying with a strand of hair, twisting it around his finger in the same way he'd done to the rest of her since the first moment she'd met him.

'I'm a busy mum. You're the high-flying CEO who plans everything to the nth degree. How long do you think it will take to organise our wedding?'

His eyes glittered with intent as he tugged gently on the strand of hair, bringing their lips mere centimetres apart.

'You'll be in hospital for five nights. So is a week from today too soon?'

'To start the rest of our lives together? Never,' she said, closing the tiny distance between them, and kissing him till they were both panting and breathless.

'I'm kidding,' he said, desire clouding his eyes in a dark fog. 'I'll give you a chance to catch your breath.'

She smiled and dropped a kiss on his lips. 'Soon is fine. A small ceremony with you, me and Maeve. Perfect.'

'Perfect,' he echoed, sliding his arms around her till she had no option but to snuggle tight against his chest, knowing she'd found what she'd always wanted.

Love, respect and validation, made all the more special by Maeve, their adorable baby girl sleeping peacefully by their side.

A family of her own.

Perfect indeed.

HARLEQUIN® *Romance*®

MEDITERRANEAN DADS

In the first of this emotional Mediterranean Dads duet,
nanny Julie is whisked away to a palatial Italian villa,
but she feels completely out of place in Massimo's
glamorous world. Her biggest challenge, though, is
ignoring her attraction to the brooding tycoon.

Look *for*

The Italian Tycoon and the Nanny

by Rebecca Winters

in March wherever you buy books.

HARLEQUIN®
Live the emotion™

® HARLEQUIN®

INTRIGUE®

THRILLER—
**Heart-pounding romance and suspense
that will thrill you long into the night....**

Experience the new THRILLER miniseries
beginning in March with:

WYOMING
MANHUNT

BY

ANN VOSS
PETERSON

Riding horseback through the Wyoming wilderness
was supposed to be the trip of a lifetime for
Shanna Clarke. Instead she finds herself running
for her life. Only rancher Jace Lantry can
help her find justice—and serve revenge.

*Available in March
wherever you buy books.*

REQUEST YOUR FREE BOOKS!
2 FREE NOVELS PLUS 2
FREE GIFTS!

HARLEQUIN ROMANCE®

From the Heart, For the Heart

YES! Please send me 2 FREE Harlequin Romance® novels and my 2 FREE gifts. After receiving them, if I don't wish to receive any more books, I can return the shipping statement marked "cancel." If I don't cancel, I will receive 4 brand-new novels every month and be billed just $3.57 per book in the U.S., or $4.05 per book in Canada, plus 25¢ shipping and handling per book and applicable taxes, if any*. That's a savings of over 15% off the cover price! I understand that accepting the 2 free books and gifts places me under no obligation to buy anything. I can always return a shipment and cancel at any time. Even if I never buy another book from Harlequin, the two free books and gifts are mine to keep forever.   114 HDN EEV7   314 HDN EEWK

Name	(PLEASE PRINT)	
Address		Apt.
City	State/Prov.	Zip/Postal Code

Signature (if under 18, a parent or guardian must sign)

Mail to the **Harlequin Reader Service®**:
IN U.S.A.: P.O. Box 1867, Buffalo, NY 14240-1867
IN CANADA: P.O. Box 609, Fort Erie, Ontario L2A 5X3

Not valid to current Harlequin Romance subscribers.

Want to try two free books from another line?
Call 1-800-873-8635 or visit www.morefreebooks.com.

* Terms and prices subject to change without notice. NY residents add applicable sales tax. Canadian residents will be charged applicable provincial taxes and GST. This offer is limited to one order per household. All orders subject to approval. Credit or debit balances in a customer's account(s) may be offset by any other outstanding balance owed by or to the customer. Please allow 4 to 6 weeks for delivery.

Your Privacy: Harlequin is committed to protecting your privacy. Our Privacy Policy is available online at www.eHarlequin.com or upon request from the Reader Service. From time to time we make our lists of customers available to reputable firms who may have a product or service of interest to you. If you would prefer we not share your name and address, please check here. ☐

HR0

HARLEQUIN *Romance*

Coming Next Month

Join Harlequin Romance® in the fairy-tale mountains of Europe,
on the shimmering Italian coast, at a grand Australian estate—
and don't be late for an engagement in the boardroom!

#4009 A ROYAL MARRIAGE OF CONVENIENCE Marion Lennox
By Royal Appointment
Life doesn't always turn out the way you plan, right? As heir to the throne,
Nikolai knows duty must always come first. But country vet Rose, his
convenient wife-to-be, is not quite what Nikolai was expecting....

#4010 THE ITALIAN TYCOON AND THE NANNY Rebecca Winters
Mediterranean Dads
In the first book of this emotional duet, nanny Julie is whisked away to
a palatial Italian villa, but feels completely out of place in Massimo's
glamorous world. Her biggest challenge, though, is ignoring her attraction
to the brooding tycoon....

#4011 PROMOTED: TO WIFE AND MOTHER Jessica Hart
Perdita's efficient, no-nonsense attitude works just fine in the boardroom.
But when she meets executive Ed, and their business relationship
becomes personal, she's left wondering whether being a wife and mother
would suit her better.

#4012 FALLING FOR THE REBEL HEIR Ally Blake
It's definitely true that opposites attract, and Kendall couldn't be more
different from Hudson Bennington III. She likes safe and secure—and he's
got danger written all over him! But then he proposes a deal, and Kendall's
tempted to accept....

#4013 TO LOVE AND TO CHERISH Jennie Adams
Heart to Heart
Sometimes we think we're better off coping with hardship alone, trying to
protect the ones we love. When Jack went away he broke Tiffany's heart,
but now that his demons are behind him, he's back—and determined to
make things right.

#4014 THE SOLDIER'S HOMECOMING Donna Alward
Shannyn's beautiful daughter is a daily reminder of her true love, Jonas,
who left town to be a soldier. Now that Jonas is back, hardened by war,
Shannyn must find a way to reach his soul again for the sake of her
daughter and the family she longs for.

HRCNM0208